They cleared the last step when a shot rang out.

Leora screamed out Fletcher's name, terrified they'd shot him.

"I'm here. I'm *oke*." His voice came from close by.

"Both of you keep quiet," the woman said and released Leora's arm. Leora swayed slightly. First, her *bruder* had gone missing, and now Ethan. After hours on the road, the hired taxi driver had brought her to Ethan's door and into a nightmare she didn't understand.

Leora inched toward the sound of Fletcher's voice while praying she wouldn't draw attention to herself. Her foot connected with a rock, and she stumbled into the solid wall of his chest.

"I've got you," Fletcher whispered and did his best to steady her despite his secured hands.

Leora pulled in several breaths and ran her clasped hands across her damp forehead. "What are they going to do with us?" she murmured for him alone.

"I don't know. But we must do whatever is necessary to stay alive."

Whatever is necessary. The words settled into her troubled thoughts. What would that entail?

Mary Alford was inspired to become a writer after reading romantic suspense greats Victoria Holt and Phyllis A. Whitney. Soon, creating characters and throwing them into dangerous situations that tested their faith came naturally for Mary. In 2012, Mary entered the speed dating contest hosted by Love Inspired Suspense and later received "the call." Writing for Love Inspired Suspense has been a dream come true for Mary.

Books by Mary Alford

Love Inspired Suspense

Forgotten Past
Rocky Mountain Pursuit
Deadly Memories
Framed for Murder
Standoff at Midnight Mountain
Grave Peril
Amish Country Kidnapping
Amish Country Murder
Covert Amish Christmas
Shielding the Amish Witness
Dangerous Amish Showdown
Snowbound Amish Survival
Amish Wilderness Survival

Visit the Author Profile page at LoveInspired.com.

AMISH WILDERNESS SURVIVAL

MARY ALFORD

LOVE INSPIRED SUSPENSE
INSPIRATIONAL ROMANCE

LOVE INSPIRED® SUSPENSE
INSPIRATIONAL ROMANCE

ISBN-13: 978-1-335-58835-7

Recycling programs
for this product may
not exist in your area.

Amish Wilderness Survival

Copyright © 2023 by Mary Eason

This is a work of fiction. Names, characters, places and incidents are either the
product of the author's imagination or are used fictitiously. Any resemblance
to actual persons, living or dead, businesses, companies, events or locales is
entirely coincidental.

For questions and comments about the quality of this book, please contact us
at CustomerService@Harlequin.com.

Love Inspired
22 Adelaide St. West, 41st Floor
Toronto, Ontario M5H 4E3, Canada
www.LoveInspired.com

Printed in U.S.A.

Thou art my hiding place; thou shalt preserve me from trouble; thou shalt compass me about with songs of deliverance. Selah.
—*Psalm* 32:7

To my wonderful readers. Your support through the years has meant the world to me. Thank you all for coming along with me on this journey back to the beautiful West Kootenai Amish community.

ONE

I have to help a friend...

Fletcher Shetler couldn't get the last words his friend said to him out of his head. At the time, he hadn't thought much about it. That was Ethan—always lending a hand to those in need. Yet the week of silence certainly wasn't like him. Far from it. Especially not with the new venture Ethan had recently embarked upon demanding so much of this time.

Training dogs for search and rescue missions into the mountains had become Ethan's passion. He'd worked with military dogs during his career in the marines and talked about how rewarding it had been. When the opportunity arose to train dogs for mountain conditions, Ethan had come to Fletcher to assist, and Fletcher was happy to help. Truth be told, he enjoyed the work.

So far, they had five young dogs going through the training process, and all were promising.

When Ethan had left, he'd assured Fletcher he'd only be gone a couple of days. The time frame had come and gone. The silence on Ethan's part was setting off all sorts of alarms in Fletcher's head.

He stared out the kitchen window at the growing clouds hovering near the mountain range near his West Kootenai, Montana, home. The shots he'd heard earlier could have come from anywhere…or they could have come from the same direction as Ethan's place. With the mountains so close, sound could be distorted by echoing off them.

Because of Fletcher and his *bruder* Mason's affiliation with the search and rescue program, the bishop in their district had allowed them to carry cell phones. Fletcher had been trying to reach his friend unsuccessfully for a couple of days.

Coming from a close-knit family with four other *bruders*, Fletcher had gotten used to looking out for those he loved, and Ethan was like family.

Still, as a former marine, Ethan Connors was more than capable of taking care of himself. He'd proved this time and again. So why was Fletcher so worried? Maybe it had been the look of concern in Ethan's eyes when he'd told Fletcher about the trip, or the fact Ethan rarely went a day without touching base with either Fletcher or Mason. Even when he'd had the flu, Ethan had checked in daily because not only was he a partner in Fletcher, Ethan and Mason's hunting guide business, but he was also a key member of the county's search and rescue team.

Now, with the cold setting in and hunting season looming, the chance of someone getting lost up in the mountains would increase dangerously with the influx of hunters roaming the countryside. Ethan would want to be around to respond to calls.

So where was he?

The knot in Fletcher's stomach wouldn't let him simply dismiss his concerns and go about his daily chores. If something had happened to his friend and he did nothing, Fletcher wouldn't be able to forgive himself.

He smacked his palms against the kitchen counter, grabbed his coat and headed out the door, the decision made. He'd ride over to Ethan's and check on the dogs; see for himself that everything was okay. Maybe Ethan had returned exhausted from his trip. That would explain why he wasn't answering any of Fletcher's calls. This was the outcome he hoped for, and yet the little niggling at the back of his mind wouldn't let him accept it.

As he saddled the horse, he could almost

picture Ethan teasing him when he showed up at his door worried about the ex-marine. The thought made Fletcher smile, yet it didn't ease his concerns.

Though Fletcher had helped Ethan build the training facility, they'd been friends for several years—since Fletcher had been introduced to Ethan through Fletcher's older *bruder* Aaron.

Ethan's love for hunting had made him a *gut* fit for the hunting guide business Fletcher and Mason had started. From there, he and Mason had joined the county's search and rescue services at Ethan's urging. When his friend had voiced his desire to train dogs for the SAR program, Fletcher had willingly agreed to assist. He was proud of the work they did for the county through the SAR program. It was fulfilling, gave him a sense of giving back to his community, as well.

While he and Ethan had worked on the training facility, his friend had shared some of the missions he'd been part of when he'd served on a special ops team. From going into a heavily guarded enemy prison to rescue a US soldier, to having to defuse a bomb seconds before it was scheduled to go off. Fletcher couldn't imagine going through such dangerous missions when the lives of his fellow soldiers, as well as others they were trying to save, were on the line.

Fletcher climbed up into the saddle and urged Jacob, the two-year-old gelding, from the barn. Once they cleared the structure, he pressed his knees against the gelding's sides. Jacob immediately responded and took off at a hard gallop.

Fall in the mountains presented its own dangers. You never knew when you'd run into a stray bear foraging for a last bit of food before going into hibernation. And sometimes the snow came early, creating havoc to those not prepared for the winter months.

Halfway to Ethan's place, the dogs could be heard barking anxiously. Something was definitely wrong. Tension worked along Fletcher's spine. He rode harder while all sorts of terrible possibilities raced through his head. The sunny day shifted overhead. A cool breeze chased down from the snowcapped mountains. Ugly clouds gathering around the peaks seemed to warn something was coming, and Fletcher wasn't sure it would be confined to the weather alone.

Once he crested the final hill, Ethan's house and barn spread out before him. Near the barn, the training facility he'd worked on always made him proud. A fine example of Amish craftsmanship that went back generations.

Yet today, his admiration was eclipsed by the mounting concern for his friend. It twisted like knives between Fletcher's shoulder blades. He'd worked with the pups long enough to be able to interpret each of their sounds. The calls coming from them now were alerting Fletcher to trouble. The only question was how bad it was going to be.

Please, Gott, *let Ethan be* oke.

Fletcher applied enough pressure with his right leg for the gelding to respond. Jacob headed left to the training facility while all sorts of bad outcomes flew through Fletcher's mind. Had something happened to Ethan inside the facility and the dogs were doing their best to bring help?

"Whoa, boy." Fletcher pulled back on the reins once they reached the building. When the horse had stopped, he hopped down and wrapped the reins around the fence post for the outdoor running pen.

Fletcher reached the gate and started to open it when something occurred to him. Molly wasn't barking her head off like the pups. The ten-year-old German shepherd had once been a military dog until she'd retired and Ethan had adopted her. Though Molly wasn't part of the training sessions, she was highly skilled. If something had happened at Ethan's place, then the dog would be sounding the alarm.

"Molly, come," he called out and waited.

After several more tries to locate the dog, his worries skyrocketed.

Molly normally stayed in the house with Ethan and had her own doggy door so she could come and go as she pleased. With the pups making so much noise, he'd expect Molly to be close.

Even if she'd gone out exploring, with all the commotion and with Fletcher calling her, Molly would come if she could.

If she could… Fletcher's own words haunted him. He quickly unlatched the gate and entered the pen. Two of the bloodhounds were outside the building in the dog run. Both stopped their barking and came over to investigate. Radar and Dakota recognized Fletcher and quieted, wagging their tails.

"What's got you all so worked up? Is Ethan in there?" If only answers could be found in those serious eyes.

He did his best to soothe the dogs, petting each one before he stepped inside the building. Right away, the rest of the dogs ceased barking. The two St. Bernard pups, Nimshi and Trackr, bounded over first. Kit, the Bluetick Coonhound, the newest dog to join the training, was a bit more hesitant. She seemed to take her cue from the rest and came over to sniff Fletcher's leg.

His gaze searched the open space where the dogs slept. There was no sign of Ethan, or any indication he'd been there recently. So, if it wasn't Ethan, then what had the dogs so worked up? Molly's absence was the most troubling concern in his opinion.

After he fed the dogs, Fletcher checked their water before leaving the building.

"Molly—come here, girl." He tried again to get the dog's attention. Fletcher scanned the countryside around the spread for any sign of the animal or anything out of place. He found neither.

The garage was on the other side of the training facility. Fletcher started for it at a rushed click while praying he would see Ethan's truck parked inside. He swung the door open. The cavernous empty space wiped away all hope that this was just a strange occurrence and the dogs had gotten themselves worked up without a *gut* reason.

Fletcher strode quickly for the house. A little way from the front entrance, he caught sight of the door standing open. Only slightly, but still…

His footsteps faltered. When he'd checked on the dogs the day before, the door had been closed. If Ethan wasn't home, then why would the door be open?

Fletcher felt inside his coat pocket; only the knife he kept with him for use around the farm. He'd left the house in a hurry and had forgotten to bring the cell phone. It wasn't something Fletcher had gotten accustomed to carrying even with the bishop's permission. Still, without the phone, there would be no way to call for help. Ethan didn't have a landline anymore.

Fletcher returned to the gelding and removed the rifle from its holster near the saddle before pocketing additional shells. The open door brought a whole new possible threat to the situation. One that warned him not to go inside unarmed.

With his heart pounding in his ears, Fletcher started for the house once more. He reached the porch and stepped up on it. What he saw on the door stopped him in his tracks. Blood. Smeared near the handle. Someone or something was hurt.

Fletcher pulled in a breath and eased through the open door. The sight inside the house confirmed he had reason to be worried. It had been torn apart. Someone had been looking for something specific.

What if the people who had destroyed Ethan's home were still here?

Fletcher's grip tightened on the rifle while he listened to the uncomfortable penetrating silence. What if the person was still there? He could be walking into a setup.

He stepped into the kitchen where drawers

had been opened, contents strewed across the counters and floor. The rest of the house proved the same state of disarray, yet so far there was no sign of the person who had done the damage or any indication Ethan had ever returned.

As a former marine who had been part of some high-level special ops missions, Ethan had told him several times that he'd made lots of enemies who wanted him dead, which was why he'd created a panic room in the house.

It was all Fletcher had left to check. If Ethan was hurt, maybe he'd used the room to escape his attackers? Hope flared for a second before Fletcher thought it through more clearly. If Ethan was hiding, he'd have seen Fletcher's approach through the monitors in the room and come out. Unless he couldn't.

Fletcher blindly ran down the hall to the entrance. He couldn't get inside the room fast enough. Once he'd pressed the wall panel where the keypad was disguised, a space on the wall flipped open. The keypad appeared. Fletcher punched in the code as fast as his fingers would slide across the keyboard. The door swung open. "Ethan? Are you here?"

Nothing but more disappointing silence. Yet something shifted in the corner of the room. Fletcher quickly flipped on the light. His hope at finding his friend safe evaporated. The person shielding their eyes against the overhead glare wasn't Ethan at all, but a woman. An Amish woman.

She slowly dropped her hand and stared at him with huge, fearful eyes.

Fletcher immediately lowered the weapon. "Who are you? Where's Ethan?"

The woman clutched her arms around her body without answering. The guarded look on her face assured him she didn't trust him enough to give answers.

"My name is Fletcher Shetler. Ethan is my friend and business partner. I won't hurt you. I promise. Can you tell me what happened here?"

The woman's clear blue eyes widened almost as if she recognized his name. Her dark red hair peeked out from beneath her traveling bonnet. It seemed to suggest she'd just arrived and hadn't had time to remove it.

As he continued to study her appearance, Fletcher's frown deepened. He didn't remember seeing a buggy outside, and he didn't recognize her from their community. How had she gotten here?

"I am Leora Mast," she said at last, her voice unsteady and barely above a whisper. "Ethan spoke of you often." She closed her eyes briefly, as if to gather her strength. "But I have no idea what happened here or where Ethan is."

Ethan spoke of him... This woman knew Ethan.

The shots he'd heard earlier were foremost on his mind. "When did you arrive here?" She appeared innocent enough, yet she was the only person inside a ransacked house, and his friend still wasn't home. He couldn't afford to dismiss anything.

Leora watched him cautiously, and he found himself a little off balance by the intensity in the depths of those eyes. "Not long. Maybe ten minutes before you arrived."

He'd heard a vehicle traveling down the road near Ethan's place. He'd been too worried about his friend to think much of it.

"I hired an Amish taxi to get here. When I walked in and saw the mess, I was worried about Ethan."

Fletcher's eyes narrowed. "How do you know Ethan?" Nothing about what he'd found so far made sense, including her and her claim of being Ethan's friend.

"My *bruder* was in his marine unit. Ethan kept in touch with Tanner and with me. We became friends through the years though we've never actually met in person. Anyway, I've been trying to reach Ethan by phone for several days now. When I couldn't get him or Tanner on the phone, I came to make sure he was *oke*."

Ethan had never mentioned this woman before. What she said about her brother sank in past the fog of fear. "Your *bruder* isn't Amish?"

Leora hesitated, as if debating how much to trust him with. "*Nay,* he left the faith many years ago. He and Ethan became close while serving together. When he couldn't reach my *bruder,* Ethan would call me at my *Englisch* employer's fabric shop. Tanner had told him if he ever needed to get in contact with him and couldn't, he should call me," she said in answer to his next question. "Tanner traveled around a lot when he left the marines. Ethan often had trouble keeping in touch, so he would call me to get an update. Over time, Ethan and I became friends. We shared a common bond—my *bruder.*" She shrugged and glanced around the room. "After I found the house in such a state and I saw you approaching, I came in here. I thought you were part of the people responsible for this mess."

"The people? How do you know there was more than one person involved?" The question came out sharper than he'd intended, but at this point he couldn't afford to blindly trust anyone, including her.

She flinched at his tone. "I don't know. I assumed there had to be more than one person involved if they were able to get to Ethan."

Get to Ethan… Was it possible Ethan had been here and then taken against his will? The idea didn't make sense. Ethan was a soldier. His vehicle wasn't in the garage. Fletcher wanted to believe his friend was still out there somewhere, waiting to return home.

"How did you get into this panic room? Ethan always leaves it closed."

Fletcher waited and watched her reaction. Was she as innocent as she appeared? As much as he wanted to believe she'd just happened here, looking for Ethan, he hadn't heard Ethan mention her before, and she claimed to be a friend. Was it simply a coincidence she was in the secured room right after Ethan's house had been ransacked? Maybe it was all those stories Ethan had talked about with some of the covert missions he'd worked on with CIA officers, but Fletcher couldn't let go of his reservations. Ethan had told him many times to never question his sense of doubt. It might be the only thing to keep you alive.

"It was open when I came in…" She stopped abruptly and touched a hand to her head, swaying slightly on her feet. "I'm sorry. It's been a very long trip from Colorado to Montana," she added when she caught his surprise.

Fletcher forgot all about his worry over Ethan and his mistrust of her. She wasn't well.

"Are you *oke*?"

She closed her eyes and dragged in several breaths, proving she was far from okay.

Fletcher covered the space between them in two strides. Leora grabbed hold of his arm to steady herself. A moment of panic showed on her face before she collapsed into his arms.

After the initial shock subsided, Fletcher carefully lowered her onto the carpeted floor. She appeared so pale. The light blue shade of her dress beneath her cloak enhanced the washed-out color.

What did he do now? He knew very little about her—only her name and that she'd come from Colorado. He skimmed her delicate features. Freckles scattered across her nose, and her eyelashes were the color of her hair. Leora's bonnet had slipped slightly sideways, revealing several curls escaped from their pins.

It had been a long time since he'd held a woman or had someone to protect—not since Catherine.

Unbidden, Fletcher recalled that final argument. Once, they'd planned to marry, until Catherine had told him she wanted more than the life he could provide for her in West Kootenai, Montana. The bottom had fallen out of his world and the life he'd envisioned for himself would never be. Since then, he'd thrown himself into work and tried to shut out those ugly words.

In his peripheral vision, something alarming jerked his attention from the unconscious woman. Movement showed on the security monitors picking up what was happening outside. Fletcher jumped to his feet and stepped closer to the monitors. There were five screens reflecting every possible angle of the property as well as each room of the house.

Through the fading daylight, several people emerged from the woods at the side of the property. All wore disguises covering their faces, and all were heavily armed.

If these were the ones who'd ransacked the house and possibly taken Ethan, perhaps they hadn't found whatever they'd been looking for. They'd see the horse and know someone was there.

Leora moaned softly. He knelt beside her. She turned her head toward him, her eyes latching onto his. "What happened?"

"You fainted. Leora, we've got trouble." He hated to alarm her, but she needed to know the danger coming after them. "There are armed men moving this way. Stay here. I'll be right back." Fletcher rushed from the room and quickly closed the keypad access panel. If you didn't know it was there, you would never guess it existed or that there was a room tucked on the other side of the wall. But Leora had said the door was open when she'd arrived, so chances are they'd have seen it already. Still, he had to do everything within his power to protect them. If it were open earlier, perhaps they wouldn't know the code to enter.

Fletcher returned to the room and closed the door. The state-of-the-art locks slid into place. Ethan had told him the room was soundproof. Those outside the walls shouldn't hear anything from inside. Still, he didn't want to test it out and realize Ethan had made a fatal mistake.

He knelt beside Leora and carefully helped her sit up. As troubling as her health issues were, what was coming their way would be a lot worse.

"We should be safe here." He kept his voice low and tried to assure her of something he didn't actually believe. No sooner had he spoken the words when the monitor confirmed the armed gunmen were closing in on the house.

Fletcher rose and helped Leora to her feet.

"They're almost here." She watched the screens with a look of horror on her face. "What have they done to Ethan and my *bruder*?"

"Your brother?" Fletcher swung toward her. "He's with Ethan?"

I have to help a friend...

She nodded. "I believe so. Ethan went to find Tanner."

Her *bruder* was the friend Ethan had been helping.

While Fletcher tried to untangle what was happening, several of the armed men fanned out across the property. Had Ethan escaped the attack? If he had, these men appeared determined to find him and make sure he didn't tell his story.

Leora clamped her hand over her mouth while panic rose, replacing the stress of the trip. She edged closer to the Amish man at her side. Though she didn't know him personally, Ethan had spoken of Fletcher as a friend. She could trust him.

Several inches taller than Tanner, his light brown hair was swept back from a wide forehead. He'd lost the straw hat he'd worn when he'd first come into the room. Leora's attention returned to the screen, where Fletcher continued to watch the nightmare unfold.

Three of the armed men entered the house.

"Someone's here. Search the entire place. Bring them to me." A woman's voice! The person giving the orders was a woman. She walked with the confidence of someone in charge.

The two men spread out, following the woman's command. Cameras positioned inside the house showed them searching through each room.

Nothing about these past two weeks and the

threats she'd endured made what was happening now a surprise.

It had all started when someone had entered her house while she'd been at work and torn it apart, much like they had Ethan's place now. Then, a man she didn't know had called the shop and demanded to know where her brother was hiding "the stuff." She'd had no idea what he was talking about and told him as much.

As soon as the call had ended, Leora had tried to reach her *bruder*, hoping he could explain. Only, Tanner hadn't answered any of her calls. Desperate, she'd turned to Ethan. Though she'd never actually met Ethan in person, she'd considered him a *gut* friend and they'd spoken frequently. Ethan knew what she'd gone through in the past and would call to check on her often.

When he'd heard what had happened, Ethan had been immediately concerned and assured her he would try to locate Tanner. He'd told her to stay with someone else until he could figure out what was happening. She had believed there was a simple explanation, and everything would be *oke*. Only, it hadn't been. Far from it.

"There's no one here."

Leora's attention jerked to the screen once more, her eyes wide with disbelief. She recognized the voice of the man speaking. He'd been one of several who'd broken into her house that final time.

As bad as those two prior incidents had been, it was the last event that had been the most terrifying.

A few days after the threatening phone call at work, several men had broken into her house wearing disguises—just like the ones now. The same person talking here was the one who had done the speaking at her home. He'd told Leora she'd had a day to return what Tanner had stolen, otherwise they'd come back and "take care" of her like they planned to do to Tanner. As hard as she'd tried to understand why they'd been accusing Tanner of taking something, it hadn't made sense. Her brother wasn't a thief. Sure, he'd gotten into a few scrapes when he was young—mostly acting out of anger or, as Leora believed, because of the horrific way their parents had died. But the marines and Ethan had straightened him out. In her opinion, what Tanner was being accused of doing went way beyond youthful anger.

After that distressing confrontation, Leora realized Ethan had been right; it hadn't been safe for her to be alone. She'd left right away for her great-aunt and -uncle's. Planning to stay awhile, she'd then tried to reach Ethan by phone and couldn't. With each failed attempt to contact her friend, Leora's fear had increased. She'd made this frantic trip from the San Luis Valley of Colorado to the West Kootenai community because she'd been terrified the men hunting Tanner might have come after Ethan.

"Whoever rode the horse must have seen us approaching and run away," the woman said. "Let's go. We're wasting our time here."

"Not so fast," the man Leora recognized said, contesting the woman. "We didn't check the panic room. The door was open before."

A chill sped down her spine. They knew about the panic room.

The woman slowly faced him. "One of our people probably shut it by accident. Let's go." She raised her voice to get the man's attention.

"Not until we check the room." The man's steely voice confirmed he was challenging her authority. "*He* won't be pleased if we let someone get away and they go to the authorities. What if it's the sister in there?"

Shockwaves chased through Leora's body. Was it possible they'd followed her here? She saw all the questions in Fletcher's eyes, and she couldn't begin to answer any of them. Not with the threat closing in.

Fletcher removed a pocketknife from his coat pocket and tucked it into his boot. He aimed the rifle toward the entrance as the man whose voice she'd recognized purposely stopped by the wall where Leora had seen Fletcher use the keypad.

"This is a waste of time," the woman insisted, but the man ignored her.

"They know the code," Fletcher said. There was only one way Leora could think of that they'd be in possession of the security code… and it meant they'd forced it from either Ethan or her *bruder*. The disturbing truth had barely cleared his lips when the door popped open and he pushed Leora behind him.

"Gun!" the man yelled and leveled his at Fletcher. "Drop it."

Leora peeked past Fletcher's shoulder as the horror unfolded.

"That's far enough," Fletcher told the intruders.

The woman ordered the man with the gun to stand down, but he didn't listen. He advanced on Fletcher, seemingly unafraid of the weapon in his hand.

Fletcher fired. All three ducked. The shot pinged off the soundproof wall.

Before Fletcher had a chance to pull the trigger, the shooter grabbed the barrel of the rifle and his second shot hit the ceiling.

While Fletcher struggled to free his weapon, the second man attacked him.

"Don't fight me," the woman snarled, grabbing Leora's arm.

A weapon pressed against Leora's head.

"Drop your weapon unless you want me to shoot her," the woman ordered Fletcher.

Leora could smell gun oil. The faint scent of gunpowder released through the bullets the weapon had fired recently.

Fletcher's eyes latched onto Leora's. "All right, I'm dropping it." He stopped struggling and slowly lowered his rifle.

"Tie them both up. Start with him." She was starting with the stronger of the two. If Fletcher was disabled, the chances of Leora escaping were small. "We'll have to take them with us."

"Or we can shoot them," the aggressor who'd attacked Fletcher said with a nasty grin. She remembered his grin, and it gave her cold shivers.

"No one's shooting anyone. That's Tanner's sister. She may know where the stuff is hidden. Let's take her along with the Amish man. He might be useful in getting her to talk."

What were they looking for? What had Tanner gotten embroiled in that had brought these dangerous people to her home and to Ethan's?

The woman lowered the gun but still clutched Leora's arm tight, forcing her to watch the two men rough-handle Fletcher. While one man kept a gun against his side, the second blindfolded

Fletcher and secured his hands in front of him with zip ties.

"Watch him while I get her hands secured." The woman shoved the weapon into the waist of her jeans. Keeping her attention on Leora's face, she secured her hands together. Was it Leora's imagination or was the woman trying to warn her of something?

As the thought worked its way through her fear-numbed brain, a blindfold was placed over her eyes, and a fuzzy blackness replaced whatever secrets the woman had been trying to convey.

"Get him outside." She kept a firm grip on Leora's arm.

"Where are you taking us?" Leora asked. "Where are my brother and Ethan?"

"Keep quiet," the woman ordered. The sharpness of her tone had Leora doubting she'd seen anything compassionate in this woman.

A cool breeze whipped Leora's dress around her legs once they reached the outdoors.

"Get the others. We're leaving. This was a waste of time." She emphasized the words she'd told the one man earlier. "Tanner didn't hide the stuff here." The woman led Leora carefully from the porch.

A shot rang out. Leora screamed out Fletcher's name, terrified they'd shot him.

"I'm here. I'm *oke*." His voice came from close by.

"Both of you keep quiet," the woman said and released Leora's arm. Leora swayed slightly. She could feel herself fading quickly. The last treatment had taken its toll on her body. Her doctor had warned about the severe fatigue. Leora couldn't imagine what he'd say if he knew she'd traveled from Colorado so soon after the final round of chemo. But what choice had she had? First, her *bruder* had gone missing and now Ethan. After hours on the road, the hired taxi driver had brought her to Ethan's door and into a nightmare she didn't understand.

Leora inched toward the sound of Fletcher's voice while praying she wouldn't draw attention to herself. Her foot connected with a rock and she stumbled into the solid wall of his chest.

"I've got you," Fletcher whispered and did his best to steady her despite his secured hands.

Leora pulled in several breaths and ran her clasped hands across her damp forehead. "What are they going to do with us?" she murmured for him alone.

"I don't know. But we must do whatever is necessary to stay alive."

Whatever is necessary… The words settled into her troubled thoughts. What would this entail?

Leora focused on the sounds around her. Off

to her right, the woman spoke to another man. She appeared angry with him.

"There's been enough shooting already. The last thing we need is to draw more unwanted attention. Gunshots have a way of carrying."

"Sorry, Jade. I thought I saw someone in the barn."

The woman's name was Jade. There was something familiar about it.

"Stop! You used my name," she snapped. "Don't ever do that again."

"Sorry, Ja— Sorry."

"Did you make sure Connors's truck is hidden so no one will find it?"

"Yes. It's hidden. Don't worry, no one's going to find it."

Leora's heart sank. Ethan had been here. These people had hidden his vehicle to try to make it seem like he wasn't home.

"Good. Bring our vehicles from their hiding spots and get them both inside. We need her to force Tanner to talk. Well, what are you waiting for? Let's get out of here before someone comes to investigate."

They had Tanner! The blood on the door sent her mind spiraling down a dark road. They needed Tanner to tell them where he'd hidden whatever it was they believed he'd taken. But

Ethan would be a liability. Were these people capable of murder? She didn't want to find out.

First one and then a second engine fired. The surveillance cameras hadn't picked them up because they'd been hidden from view. The vehicles pulled up closer. Next, several footsteps headed toward Leora and Fletcher.

"Stay calm. Don't do anything to make them angry," Fletcher said to her.

"Let's go." Leora was yanked away from Fletcher's grasp. She recognized the voice of the man who had spoken Jade's name. Another weapon bit into her back. He grabbed her arm and forced her along while Leora's panicked brain imagined all sorts of terrible things.

"Get in there." He pushed her hard. Her legs struck something and she fell forward. Her bound hands collided with a seat. The man shoved her inside and against someone else.

"It's me." Fletcher's deep voice reached out to her. How could he sound so calm?

"I'm so scared," she breathed unsteadily.

Someone else got in beside her. "No talking. Keep your mouths shut," the same gunman warned.

Leora tried to recall the number of people she'd seen on the monitors. At least ten, which explained the multiple vehicles. She and Fletcher were far outnumbered.

Dread settled over her shoulders like a second cloak. She and Fletcher were now hostages in a situation that went much deeper than what either of them understood.

Fletcher clasped his fingers with hers. "We're *oke*."

"I said no talking." The man beside her nudged the weapon into her ribs.

Leora so wanted to believe Fletcher's assurances, but her world had been turned upside down, and she still had no idea why.

She kept as far away from the gunman as possible. Still holding Fletcher's fingers, she leaned against him and tried to calm down.

"Stay as quiet as you can," Fletcher whispered against her ear. "I'm going to try to determine where they're taking us."

She clung to the promise in those words when all she could think about was that they were at the mercy of armed thugs who had probably taken Ethan hostage, as well, and she had no idea what they'd done to her brother.

TWO

They'd left the community—this much he knew for certain. From the glimpses of countryside visible beneath his blindfold and the turns the driver made, Fletcher was positive they were heading straight into the thick of the nearby Kootenai National Forest. There were over two million acres contained there. Miles and miles of wilderness that would make it easy to get lost, and just as easy to make someone disappear.

He did his best to contain the fear. Leora was counting on him to get them out of whatever it was that was actually happening, yet he had no idea where to even begin.

Fletcher realized he still held Leora's hand as best he could with the restraints. They'd been thrown together unexpectedly. He'd do whatever necessary to keep her safe, even if it meant risking his own life to protect hers.

Without a doubt, these mercenaries had taken Ethan and Tanner. He'd overheard the woman talking about hiding Ethan's vehicle. *We need her to force Tanner to talk.* Fletcher didn't want to think about what type of torture they'd use on Leora to "force" Tanner to talk.

He tilted his head slightly. Through the sliver of a gap at the bottom of the blindfold, trees passed by outside his window. He believed they were traveling down one of the many backcountry roads leading deeper into the forest.

Fletcher faced forward. Though no one in the vehicle had spoken since the man had threatened Leora, there was the driver and someone beside him. Another man sat next to Leora. Fletcher was pretty sure he'd heard a couple more moving around in the third-row seating behind them. A second vehicle likely carried the rest of the men who had been at Ethan's property. Too many for them to fight alone.

The driver slowed. Fletcher leaned his head back and tried to see above the person seated in front of him. Headlights illuminated the space beyond the hood of the vehicle. Their captors had definitely used a less-traveled road to avoid drawing suspicion to themselves. It wouldn't do to have a passerby spot two blindfolded people and call the sheriff's office.

After they'd traveled only a short amount of time, the vehicle turned left. Trees populated both sides of the road.

Before he'd become friends with Ethan, Fletcher hadn't realized the necessity of using all of one's senses, but Ethan had trained both him and Mason in the skills he'd learned as a marine. He said it would be helpful with their search and rescue missions since, as Ethan was fond of saying, some people disappeared because they didn't want to be located. Still, others because someone was determined they wouldn't be found.

For Fletcher, the leap from hunting guide to being part of the SAR team had come naturally. Both Fletcher and Mason had been hunting the woods and the mountains surrounding the West Kootenai community all their lives. He'd felt as if he could use that knowledge to search for those who were injured and lost. He was proud of the work they did through the SAR program. Each person they were able to save made it possible for him or her to return to their families. It was a *gut* feeling.

The vehicle jostled along the pitted road. Fletcher heard the sound of mud being slung underneath the SUV along with water splashing up from the earlier rains. Fletcher didn't know if Leora had told anyone where she was going, but he hadn't. An oversight he greatly regretted now. Mason and his family were traveling and wouldn't be home for a couple of days. Fletcher hadn't wanted to pull any of his other *bruders* into what at the time he'd assumed was nothing more than a bad feeling. In other words, no one on his end would be looking for him.

The vehicle came to a stop. They'd reached their destination. Dread settled around him. Leora seemed to realize it, too; her fingers squeezed his. From beneath his blindfold, he glimpsed nothing but woods in front of them before the driver killed the lights.

Fletcher's door opened. Someone grabbed his arm and pulled him from Leora's grasp and out of the vehicle.

"No!" Leora screamed.

He tried to free himself from the person holding him, but the grip tightened painfully.

Doors slammed shut.

"Move." Fletcher was forced along by his captor. Several people followed. Where was Leora?

"Get in there." The man pulling him shoved Fletcher forward. He stumbled over a step. Went flying across space and hit a wooden floor hard.

Sounds of a struggle followed by the door closing and a lock sliding into place.

Fletcher scrambled to his feet. "Leora." Had he and Leora been separated to interrogate them?

"I'm here." Relief came quickly. Her shaky response appeared near the door.

"Are you hurt?" It infuriated him to think of those men treating her badly.

"*Nay*, I'm *oke*."

Before he made a single step toward her, another dreadful thought occurred. What if they weren't alone in here? Fletcher listened closely. Several voices outside appeared to be discussing something. Jade's was one. She'd ordered a man to stand guard outside the shed because she needed to speak to *him*. The way she said the word led Fletcher to believe this mystery man was the real person in charge.

Using his bound hands, Fletcher worked the blindfold free from his eyes.

Blackness greeted him. Slowly, his eyes adjusted. They were in what appeared to be a small storage building. Three of the walls were lined with shelves filled with jars and canned goods. It looked as if someone had stored broken-down pieces of furniture there, as well.

He felt his way over to Leora. She gasped when he touched her and jumped back, startled.

"Sorry," he whispered. "It's hard to see in the dark. Can you get your blindfold free?"

"I think so." Leora carefully worked it free. Her frightened eyes latched onto his, reflecting the depth of what they'd been through. He wanted to hold her and reassure her they were safe, but nothing could be further from the truth.

Those people represented danger, and it was only a matter of time before someone returned to reveal their true purpose for taking them.

"I'm so worried," she whispered. "So very worried. They have my *bruder*."

"I know. I'm worried, too. But we have each other, and we can't give up. Tanner and Ethan need us to find a way out so we can help them."

"But how? The door's locked and there's a guard."

"I have an idea." He leaned down and pulled his pocketknife from his boot. The men had taken his rifle away, but they hadn't searched him or Leora. They'd probably thought, since they were Amish, they wouldn't present a threat. The knife was a necessary tool around the farm, and Fletcher always carried it with him. It had come in handy as a hunting guide's tool more times than he could count. Now, it might be the thing to save their lives.

He quickly snapped the restraints from Leora's hands before handing her the knife.

She positioned the knife against the plastic zip tie around his wrist. Soon, he was free, as well.

He rubbed his wrists where the ties had been secured too tight. "Let's see if we can find a way out of here while there's still time." He got a good look at her exhausted features and became worried. "How are you feeling?" She didn't look well, and they'd been through a lot already.

Leora dismissed his concerns with the wave of her hand. "I'm fine. The trip from Colorado was a grueling one, and we haven't exactly had time to catch our breaths."

He believed there was more to it than what she said and prayed she would be able to keep up once they did escape. They'd be on foot. Fletcher had a vague idea where they were; regardless, there would be a long walk ahead of them to get help.

"We can't draw their attention," Fletcher said loud enough for only her to hear. "Let's start in the back."

With Leora at his side, Fletcher started easing along the cluttered shed. Several times, his foot pushed through the flooring. Pieces of it had rotted away over time. He didn't want to think about what critters might be living in the shed. A large hole in the roof—too high to reach—displayed dark skies. The clouds from earlier were still hanging on.

"What's going on in there?" the man guarding yelled out when Fletcher's foot smashed through the floor once more and he couldn't cover the sound.

Fletcher froze and kept as still as possible.

Several seconds ticked by. The man didn't appear to be concerned enough to investigate.

"There's no way out other than through the front door," Fletcher said with disappointment. They'd reached the rear of the building, and the truth became clear. "We'll have to find a way to get the guard inside and overpower him."

Leora repeatedly shook her head. "We can't. It's too dangerous."

Fletcher understood her fear, but if they stayed, he had no doubt they would eventually die. "It's the only way. They will kill us at some point. Trust me, Leora. Please."

He watched the war going on through her eyes before she slowly nodded. "I do trust you."

With Leora holding on to his arm, Fletcher reached the front of the shed while being as quiet as possible. He searched for something to use as a weapon. Several table legs were scattered around the floor.

"We'll need something to restrain him once he's incapacitated." He looked around at the piles of junk for anything they could use.

"I see some rope." Leora pointed to one of the tables. A length of rope peeked out from beneath several boxes. Fletcher carefully pulled the rope out of the pile. It was old and not in the best condition, but it would have to do.

Near the door stood an old wooden barrel.

Stuff was piled on top of it. Maybe if he turned the barrel over, it would make enough noise for the man to come investigate without alerting the others.

"Go over by the window and don't make a sound. I'll get his attention."

Once Leora was in place, Fletcher grabbed the table leg and then kicked the barrel over. It landed on its side with a thud before shattering into a dozen different pieces. Like everything else in the place, it had slowly rotted away.

"What's going on in there?" the guard repeated. He sounded like he was right outside the door. Fletcher stepped to where he would be behind the door when it opened and waited while praying *Gott* would encourage the man to investigate.

Seconds ticked by. The man grumbled under his breath, then a key was inserted into the lock. This was it.

Fletcher raised the table leg into position while his hands shook. The door squeaked open. He barely waited until the man was inside before he struck hard, slamming the leg against his head. The guard crumpled without a word, unconscious halfway outside the shed.

Fletcher dropped the table leg and grabbed the guard's arms. "Help me get him inside."

They had to get him out of sight before someone came to investigate.

Leora clasped his feet. Together they pulled
the unconscious watchman inside.

"Let's get him tied up before he wakes."
Fletcher took his knife and cut the rope into
two lengths, securing the unconscious man's
hands and then his legs.

A search of his pockets yielded no cell phone
and nothing useful, not even a flashlight.

"We have to hurry, but we can't let him alert
the others. We need to give ourselves a chance
to put space between us and these men." He
looked around the floor. "I need something to
use as a gag."

"The blindfold." Leora grabbed one of their
blindfolds from the floor and handed it to him.
Fletcher quickly secured the cloth so it would
muffle any sound he made. They stepped out
into the cold night air, which was damp with
impending rain. Leora clutched her cloak closer
around her body.

An old barn sat back some distance from
where they'd been held. Beyond it, a house. A
dim light shone beyond the curtains. Fletcher
had no doubt the rest of the armed thugs would
be held up inside.

Were they still in the Kootenai National Forest? Fletcher remembered reading in the past

that there were several pieces of private property within the forest where people lived.

He indicated the woods spreading out in front of them. Once they reached the trees, Fletcher took a second to get his bearings. He was almost certain if they kept going in this direction, they'd eventually hit the road that had brought them here.

"We have to find a phone as fast as possible." With only a general idea of where they'd been taken, he prayed somewhere along the road they would run across a house with someone willing to help them.

As much as he wanted to slow down for Leora's sake, if they were caught again, it would end badly.

While they traversed the heavily treed space in front of them, Fletcher listened in the direction of the house. So far, it didn't appear as if they'd discovered the man in the shed. But for how long?

Leora's labored breathing worried him. He kept remembering how she'd fainted earlier. Something told him this was more than physical exhaustion.

"I see the road." She nodded ahead.

It appeared through the trees. A welcome relief. Before they reached it, he stopped. "Why don't you take a moment to catch your breath and wait here? I'm going to take a look down the road and make sure no one is coming."

She grabbed his arm before he could leave. "No, don't leave me."

Fletcher covered her hand with his. "I'm not. I'm going to check and see if it's safe to keep going. Take a moment to rest. I'll be right back." She slowly nodded. Leora probably hadn't faced anything like this before. He wished he hadn't. Fletcher had assisted his older *bruder* Aaron when dangerous men had come to the community looking for Aaron's wife. More recently, his younger brother Hunter and his *fraa*, Hope, had been forced to endure numerous attacks by outsiders. It was sad to say, but there had been many incidents where the outside world and its dangers had entered their formerly peaceful community.

Once he'd stepped from the trees, Fletcher headed down to the road. Pitch-black night made it almost impossible to see anything. The scent of rain clung heavily in the air. In the distance, lightning flashed. He waited through the thunder and listened closely. No sound of anyone else out here but them. Still, best to keep moving.

If they followed the road, he was almost certain they'd eventually run into a house or a business with a phone.

After a final search of his surroundings, Fletcher returned to Leora. "I don't see anyone coming along the road." He clasped her hand to help her down the steep slope.

Together they started walking while keeping close to the tree line in case their captors should discover their absence and come looking. They were heading in the opposite direction from the house. Hopefully, they would be able to cover a lot of space before anyone figured out they were gone.

"Look—over there." Leora pointed up ahead.

In the distance, a mailbox appeared by the side of the road. Past it, a driveway had been cut from the trees. "I sure hope someone lives there."

It wouldn't do them much good to make it to a vacant house because he seriously doubted there would be a landline to call for help. Better to find an occupied home. The adrenaline pouring through his body made it impossible to relax. Every little sound had him jerking toward it.

"Keep your eyes open," he warned as they started for the mailbox. Before they reached it, headlights appeared behind them.

Fletcher hurried her away from the road and into the trees. Had the driver seen them?

The headlights grew closer. Fletcher tugged her behind a large tree when he realized there was more than one set. The first vehicle eased past. An SUV—just like the one they'd been brought here in. He'd managed to see the vehicle through the bottom of the blindfold. Too big of a coincidence for it not to be their kidnappers.

A moment later, a second SUV trailed past.

"Do you think they saw us?" Leora kept her attention on the final vehicle until it was out of sight.

"They don't appear to be stopping, so I'm guessing not." He gave the SUVs a little more time before they left their hiding spot and returned to the road.

There were still lots of things he didn't understand about what was happening. He hoped Leora could give him answers. "What had you so worried about your *bruder* enough to reach out to Ethan in the first place? How is Tanner connected to what's happening now?"

Leora took her time answering. When her silence stretched on, he glanced sideways at her.

"Tanner is my twin," she said quietly. Leora told him about her *bruder*'s restless life since leaving the faith. "I tried to reach Tanner several times and couldn't. I became worried and called Ethan."

Her answer didn't really tell him anything useful. "But something specific must have happened to bring you here." He hated pressing her hard, but so far, Fletcher felt as if he were completely in the dark. He wanted to know what they were up against.

"You're right. Something did." Leora told him about the men who'd come to her house and demanded she give back what Tanner had taken. "Fletcher, I recognized one of the men's voices from earlier at Ethan's. At least one of them was at my house in Colorado."

Fletcher couldn't believe what she'd said. Who were these men, and what were they after?

"I have no idea what they're looking for, but I know Tanner wouldn't take something not belonging to him." She looked back over her shoulder to make sure no one else was coming. "After my *bruder* left the service, he traveled around a lot. Tanner struggled to fit into any job until he was hired by a transportation company. The change in him was amazing. He had a purpose. Tanner told me many times about how much he enjoyed the job." She lifted her palms. "I have no idea what's really going on."

Obviously, these people believed Tanner had taken something. To go to such extremes as kidnapping meant that whatever it was, it had to involve something illegal. "Why did your *bruder* leave the faith?" he asked once they reached the drive. Though not unheard of, most Amish chose to remain in the Plain life after their *Rumspringa*.

Fletcher glanced down the driveway. Overhanging trees left him with a sinking feeling. The house didn't look as if it had been used in a while.

"Our parents died in a fire." Her voice stumbled over the words. "I think he couldn't stay Amish and live with the memories of what he'd lost. And so, he left. It was later determined the fire was intentionally set by someone we knew." She stopped speaking.

"That must have been hard." Fletcher remembered the pain he'd experienced after losing *Daed*. It felt as if the grief had infused in his bones. Even today—after so many years—there were times when the pain would hit like a wave and knock him off his feet.

"It was for both of us. I blamed myself for…"

"For what? The fire wasn't your fault."

She swallowed deeply. "Their deaths affected Tanner in particular. He and our *daed* were close. After *Daed* and *Mamm* passed, Tanner changed." She appeared to be reflecting on the past. "Our grandparents brought us to Colorado to get away from the memories, which were everywhere in our Ruby Valley, Montana community. And we had other family in Colorado," she added when he watched her face.

As they started down the drive, something encouraging caught his eyes. A set of tire tracks, and they were recent. He stopped dead. What if it was their captors? The thought was chilling, but at this point, they needed help quickly.

"What's wrong?" Leora's full attention was on his face.

"Nothing." He didn't want to pile onto her concerns. Gott, *keep us protected.* "This happened right before Tanner joined the military?"

Leora nodded. It seemed like a strange move for someone who had once been a pacifist to join the military but certainly not unheard of. His *bruder* Mason had joined the US Marshals for a time before returning to the faith.

"Though I didn't understand it, he seemed excited about the prospect of protecting his country." She shook her head. "Yet all I did was worry that he'd be killed, and I would lose my *bruder.*"

"It must have been difficult for you."

Something changed in her expression. "It consumed my life. If only I had…"

Once more he wondered what she hadn't told him.

"You never married?" He realized he'd overstepped right away. "I'm sorry. I don't know why I asked."

"It is *oke.* I guess it just never worked out for me," she murmured.

Yet he wondered if it were the truth. He'd

used the same excuse a lot recently. Ever since the woman he'd loved had taken his heart and smashed it beyond repair. Maybe Leora's heart had been broken, too.

Lightning flashed again. Fletcher counted off three seconds until the thunder responded. It was getting closer. He didn't relish the idea of getting caught in the rain.

Leora snugged her cloak around her shoulders as a cool breeze kicked up. "After those men came to my house, I knew Tanner was in a lot of trouble—and so was I." She looked his way. "This is all my fault. I think these are part of the same people looking for whatever they think Tanner took." She stopped walking and faced him. "Somehow, these people must have followed me. I'm the one who led them here, Fletcher. Because of me, your life is in danger."

She'd brought this trouble to Fletcher's door. If she hadn't gotten Ethan involved, he might be safe now. Instead, he was missing. From the state of his house, whatever had happened there was bad. If Ethan had died because she'd sent him after Tanner, how could she ever forgive herself?

"It isn't your fault, Leora—none of it. You are not responsible for what bad men choose to do." He looked deep into her eyes and, for the first time since she'd started this frightening trip, Leora wasn't so afraid. She wasn't alone.

Fat raindrops begin to fall, spattering against her face. "Ugh. We'd better keep moving. I sure hope we find someplace to get out of the weather." It didn't take long to soak through her bonnet. She huddled beneath her cloak. Putting one foot in front of the other had become harder. Her broken body was all out of strength.

"I've got you." Fletcher put his arm around her waist, as if sensing she was in danger.

Through the trees, lights appeared up ahead. "Look. Someone's home." Leora gestured to them.

"Thank You, *Gott*," Fletcher said with enthusiasm.

She prayed the owner wouldn't be too afraid to let them in, because they really needed help.

They left the driveway and headed through the trees to reach the house faster. Lights appeared in several windows. It was a small, single-story farmhouse like so many others, whether Amish or *Englisch*.

Leora kept close to Fletcher as they climbed the steps and stood before the door. He raised his hand to knock.

"No, wait." She stopped him.

His troubled expression turned her way. "What is it? Did you hear something?"

She couldn't explain it. Maybe just the effects of what they'd gone through so far. "No, I didn't hear anything." She shook her head. "It's nothing—I'm not sure."

His gaze softened. "We're safe for now, but Ethan and Tanner are not. Let's see if we can borrow the phone and maybe warm up a bit. If anything feels off, we'll leave immediately. *Oke*?"

She trusted him. Though she barely knew Fletcher, he'd done everything in his power to protect her against immeasurable circumstances. She understood why Ethan spoke so highly of Fletcher when he'd mentioned his Amish friend. No matter what happened, they were in this together.

Leora slowly nodded. "You're right. We need help."

Fletcher smiled and tucked her hand in his. He knocked a couple of times and waited through several minutes of silence while her imagination went wild.

"No one's answering." Fletcher frowned and knocked a second time. This time, something stirred inside the house. Footsteps headed their way.

Leora's grip tightened on Fletcher's hand.

The porch light came on. Locks disengaged and the door slowly opened while Leora bit her bottom lip to hold back a panicked scream.

But the person in front of them wasn't a scary villain. Or, at least, he didn't appear to be. He was clean-cut and young—probably in his twenties. "Hello. Can I help you?" He glanced from Fletcher to Leora's soaked appearance.

"My name is Fletcher Shetler and this is Leora Mast. We're in trouble, and we need to use your phone, please."

The young man's eyes widened. He glanced beyond them, as if looking for bad guys to materialize before his attention returned to them. "You both look like you're freezing." He shook his head. "Sorry, where are my manners? Please come inside. I'll get you some towels. Name's Sam, by the way."

He stuck his hand out and Fletcher shook it. "Nice to meet you, Sam."

Sam nodded to Leora before he headed down a long hallway.

"He doesn't seem like a bad guy, does he?" she whispered, her attention on Fletcher's face. She needed to hear him agree with her.

"You're right. He doesn't. Let's go inside where it's warm." He placed his hand on her elbow. Together they stepped across the threshold. Fletcher closed the door to shut out the cold rain.

Despite his reassurances, Leora couldn't let go of her concerns. Everything they'd gone through so far screamed not to let her guard down.

She looked around at the simple furnishings. There was nothing fearful here. In the living room, a fire burned in the fireplace. Leora went over and held her hands close to the fire. There were knickknacks on the mantel and on the bookshelves. Photos of family members, she guessed. The house seemed kind of dated for someone as young as Sam. Perhaps he lived here with his parents or grandparents.

"Here you go." She jerked around at the sound of Sam's voice.

He noticed her nervous reaction. "Sorry, I didn't mean to startle you." He handed them each a towel.

"Thank you," Leora managed to say. She took the towel and began drying her face.

"Of course." Sam smiled. "Let me put another log on the fire." He grabbed one from next to the fireplace and tossed it on. Sparks flew all around.

At last, warmth began to penetrate her chilled skin. Leora removed her bonnet and did her best to dry off.

"I'm glad I was here. I arrived home from work a short time before you showed up." This explained the fresh tire tracks. Leora relaxed a little more. Nothing but an innocent curiosity showed on Sam's face when he asked what happened.

Leora glanced at Fletcher before telling him. "We were kidnapped."

"You're kidding," Sam exclaimed, his eyes wide with surprise. "Who would do such a thing?"

"I don't know." Leora did her best to explain the nightmare she and Fletcher had gone through.

"I can't believe there are such people around in this area. I've lived here in this place since I was a child, and there are only a few houses around. The property you mentioned has been vacant for quite some time."

It would make the perfect place to bring someone you'd kidnapped. "We believe they are out there looking for us now," she told him in an urgent tone. "I'm afraid there isn't much time. We need to call the police right away."

Sam's frown creased his forehead. "You think they'll come here?"

"We're not sure."

As much as Leora wished she could tell him no, she believed their captors couldn't afford to let them go. They were looking for something important, and they believed Leora could help them find it. They'd search every property along the way. Eventually, they'd come to Sam's place. She and Fletcher needed to be long gone before this happened.

THREE

"Do you mind showing me where your phone is so I can call for help?" Fletcher asked again when Sam appeared to be paralyzed by his fear.

He slowly snapped out of it. "Yes, of course. I'm sorry. It's just this is all so unbelievable." Sam shook his head. "The phone's in the kitchen. I'll show you to it." He led them from the living room and warmth of the fire.

Immediately, Fletcher felt the chill return as they walked down the hallway lined with photos of people who didn't really resemble Sam.

Was this Sam's house, or had it belonged to someone else? *I've lived here in this house with my grandparents since I was a child...* What Sam had said earlier niggled at Fletcher's brain. If he'd lived here with his grandparents, where were they?

Before he could find a nice way to ask the question, Sam stepped into the kitchen and pointed. "The phone's over by the basement door. I lost my cell phone a few days ago." He grinned sheepishly. "So far, it hasn't turned up, but the landline is hanging on the wall. Sorry it's a little old-fashioned, but my grandparents owned the house, and I haven't had the heart to upgrade since they passed."

Relief swept through Fletcher's limbs. The house had belonged to Sam's grandparents, which explained the old-fashioned furnishings. The dated photos.

Fletcher spotted the yellow phone on the wall. *"Denki."* He headed for the phone while keeping Leora close. The sooner he made the call to Sheriff Collins, the better he'd feel. He wasn't completely sure they were still within Sheriff Collins's jurisdiction, but he knew the man well. The sheriff wouldn't hesitate to assist and alert the proper authorities.

"Hang on a second. Let me turn on some more light." Sam opened the basement door and flipped on the light switch. "It's always dark over here in the corner."

As much as Fletcher wanted to believe this was almost over, the knot in his stomach kept churning and wouldn't let him relax. He lifted the receiver from its cradle and froze. No dial tone. He tried again with the same results.

Fletcher spun toward Sam. "It's not working."

Sam didn't appear surprised. "Really?" He

came closer and took the receiver from Fletcher. Sam slowly placed it in its cradle without listening for a dial tone. "Oh, well. Maybe the weather has taken down the phone lines."

But the weather had only begun to enter the area. Could it really be responsible? Something was wrong. Fletcher's gaze locked with Leora's. "We have to leave," he whispered.

Before Fletcher had taken a single step, Sam shoved him hard. He registered Leora's panicked scream before he stumbled forward...toward the open basement door. Another shove sent him tumbling down the stairs. Panicked, Fletcher tried to grab the banister—the wall—anything to stop his fall, but he couldn't get his balance enough to catch himself or slow his momentum. It felt as if he hit each stair along the way until he landed hard on the bottom step and lost consciousness briefly.

When he came to, his body hurt everywhere. Blurry images were all that appeared at first. He shook his head and then grabbed it as pain shot from the point where he'd hit it on the cement floor. A low moan escaped. He tried to move and realized something was on top of him. The weight shifted and left his body.

"Fletcher. Are you hurt?" Leora. She'd landed on top of him. He groaned and attempted to sit up.

While Fletcher tried to bring his muddled

thoughts together, the light extinguished and the door above slammed shut. Locks slid into place. One thing became frighteningly clear. Sam was not the nice young man they'd both believed. He must be working for the people who had kidnapped them.

"I'm not sure," he muttered while shaking his head to try to rid it of the cobwebs. His shoulder hurt badly, and his head was bleeding where he'd cracked it on the floor.

Fletcher rose unsteadily to his feet and grabbed the stair post with his uninjured arm. He waited until his stomach stopped heaving before he asked Leora if she was injured.

"I think I sprained my wrist." She cradled the injured arm against her chest. "Fletcher, if Sam is working with the others, and I'm almost certain of it, he'll call them. We have to find a way out of here."

She was right. They wouldn't have long. "Wait here." Ignoring the pain in his body, Fletcher felt his way up the stairs and flipped on the light. The room illuminated, revealing a large, cluttered space.

He reached the bottom step, where Leora waited. "Maybe there's another exit."

He and Leora stumbled over boxes without finding a second door.

"We'll have to go out through those." He

pointed to windows above their head, reflecting the downpour that hadn't let up. "Help me find something to stand on." Working together, they searched through the years of clutter and found a table. Getting the heavy piece of furniture where they needed it was difficult with his shoulder and Leora's injured wrist, but they managed to shove it over beneath the window.

Fletcher climbed up and tried to force the window free with his good hand. "It won't budge. We're going to have to break it. I'll need something heavy."

"Hang on." Leora searched the room and found an old radio.

"That'll work. Stand back and cover your eyes." Fletcher turned his head aside and slammed the radio against the glass. It shattered on the first attempt. Shards flew all around him, nicking his hand and face.

When the last of the glass settled, he looked at the damage. The window was mostly gone, leaving just a screen.

"Hurry, Fletcher. There's no way Sam didn't hear the window breaking."

Fletcher dropped the radio and shoved the screen hard. It took several times before it flew free.

He held out his hand for her to take. Leora climbed up beside him. "I'll go first." Fletcher removed the last of the glass fragments and heaved himself up to the window ledge. As he swung his leg over the open frame, he banged his injured shoulder and clamped down on his bottom lip to keep from shouting out.

Fletcher swung his remaining leg over the frame and stepped from the window. His foot slipped on the soggy slope of the ground, his ankle twisting beneath him. It took everything inside not to shriek in pain.

Fletcher staggered to his feet. The moment he put weight on the injured ankle, he winced. Another injury to slow them down when they didn't have a second to lose. Walking wouldn't be easy, but there was no other choice. As soon as they had a chance to catch their breaths, he'd take a look at his injuries and Leora's wrist. Until then, he'd have to deal with the pain as best he could.

By now, Sam would have contacted Jade. They'd know he had them. Their opportunity to escape was closing quickly. Injuries or not, they had to keep moving. The alternative could mean death.

"Hurry, Leora. There's not much time."

Leora glanced over her shoulder and saw Sam coming her way. Time was up.

She quickly slipped through the opening and onto the ground.

"This way." Fletcher headed them toward the nearby woods.

She noticed Fletcher favored his right leg. "You're limping."

He kept her uninjured hand in his and didn't stop when they reached the trees. "I landed wrong. It's only a sprain. Let's keep moving."

Though he tried to dismiss the pain, she could see it on his strained face. Along with his shoulder and head, Fletcher's injuries were growing.

"I can't believe Sam was involved. He seemed so sincere." Leora glanced over her shoulder. "Do you think he'll come after us or wait for the others?"

"Without a doubt, he'll be looking for us." His words were not what she wanted to hear but exactly what she believed. "He let us get away. The woman Jade and whoever she is working for won't be happy."

Even though they hadn't been walking for a long time, Leora struggled to get enough air into her lungs. She had to keep pushing past the exhaustion. Fletcher was doing everything in his power to save them, fighting through great pain. She would do the same.

The chill once more bore into her bones. Leora wiped rain from her face to see the path ahead. She didn't want to think about what might have happened to Tanner and Ethan. The guilt she felt over involving Ethan and Fletcher in this nightmare returned. If she hadn't called Ethan, would any of this be happening?

As much as she prayed this would all end once these people had whatever they thought Tanner had taken, she didn't believe it. They'd eliminate Tanner and anyone else who stood between them and freedom.

Driving rain soaked their clothes quickly. She couldn't stop shivering. They wouldn't be able to keep going like this for long.

Fletcher stopped for a second and listened. "I hear something."

Leora focused hard on what he heard. Rustling—coming from nearby. She whirled in time to see a large dog emerge from the woods and bound toward them in attack mode. "Oh, no." She shrank against Fletcher.

"Molly!" Fletcher exclaimed in a shocked tone. He recognized the dog right away. "It's okay, girl. It's me." The dog responded to his voice and changed her demeanor. "This is Ethan's dog." Fletcher leaned down and examined the dog. The German shepherd had a bloody gash on her head. "She's been hit with something. They probably knocked the dog out to get to Ethan."

Molly wagged her tail, excited to see a friendly face.

"How did she get here?" Leora asked in amazement.

Fletcher frowned. "The dog wasn't at the house when I arrived." He turned to Leora. "I think she followed the men who took Ethan and your *bruder*."

The dog sniffed the ground as if searching for her owner's scent.

"The wilderness isn't far from Ethan's place," Fletcher told her. "Molly is a trained military dog. She's been tracking Ethan. The fact that Molly is here seems to confirm Ethan was at one time. If Molly is out in the woods, she's on Ethan's trail. Which means he must have found a way to escape his captors, as well."

She prayed he had Tanner with him. Before she could voice her hope aloud, another far more disturbing sound grabbed her attention. Multiple vehicles were moving up Sam's driveway.

"They're coming to search for us." There wasn't a second to spare. With Molly sniffing the air, they pushed deeper into the woods.

The dog quickly trained on a particular trail and started through the woods at a fast run.

"I sure hope she's trained on either Ethan or your *bruder*'s scent."

If Tanner was with Ethan, her friend would protect him. She clung to the hope both Ethan and Tanner were still alive.

The rain came down in sheets, making it hard to see anything, even the dog in front of them. She had no idea how many more bad men were around the area looking for them, but they were far outnumbered, and she didn't want to think about what might happen if they were captured again.

Leora looked over her shoulder. Several flashlights had entered the woods behind them. Her heart sank. "They're following our footprints. What do we do?"

"We can't outrun them. We have to find a place to hide until they've passed by." It was a long shot, and she knew it. Chances were, if the men were tracking their steps, there would be no getting away.

Fletcher commanded the dog to stop.

Leora searched the woods for a place to hide out of sight. All she saw was more trees. With so many looking for them, and with Sam giving them the direction they'd gone, where could they possibly hide that they wouldn't be found?

Gott, we need Your help. Because she wasn't sure how much longer either of them would survive without it.

"Over there," Fletcher whispered close to her ear. "There's a downed tree. It's our only chance." He grabbed hold of Molly's collar and led her over to the rotted tree covered in moss.

The ground around it was littered with decaying branches, which should hopefully hide their footprints.

Leora crouched behind it.

"It's not going to be enough to keep us hidden from view," Fletcher said and scanned their surroundings. "There's plenty of brush around. If we can cover ourselves with it, they might not see us. Molly, stay." The dog obeyed the command as she'd been trained to do.

Working quickly, they gathered as much brush as possible. Fletcher helped her pile the brush all around and on top. It was risky. If they were spotted, there would be no escaping. He'd then walked deeper into the woods and circled back around to create a deception that he and Leora had kept going.

With Molly crouching beside them, Leora wrapped her arms around Fletcher and prayed this decision wouldn't be another among the many wrong ones she'd made that would lead to their deaths.

Fletcher gestured for the dog to lie down and she obeyed.

Tucked in close beside Fletcher, Leora tried to hear anything above the drumming of her heart.

"They have a dog with them. Are we sure this is our people?" An unknown man clearly had doubts thanks to Molly's appearance.

"It's them," Sam said. "The one footprint is much smaller. I don't know where the dog came from, but these footprints belong to them. And they're getting away. I can't let them escape like I let Tanner and the other fellow. He'll kill me if this happens. With the rain picking up, it won't be long before their footprints are washed away. Let's go."

Tanner and Ethan had escaped. Leora held on to the hope they'd reach law enforcement in time to stop whatever these men had planned.

Fletcher still held Leora tight while she thought about what Sam had said. He'd mentioned a man—like Jade had before. There was someone higher up calling the shots.

Leora's thoughts yanked back to the moment when several sets of footsteps could be heard moving through the woods.

Their pursuers fanned out around the tree trunk, their flashlights flooding the area.

Gott, keep us hidden. The prayer slipped through her head as her eyes followed the flashlight beams.

"The underbrush is so thick through here, I can't find their tracks again." A different male voice from the others.

"Well, they can't have disappeared," Sam yelled. A flashlight shot toward the tree stump and Leora did her best not to react. "Let's keep going. They're probably hurt from tumbling down the stairs. We should be able to catch them."

When the lights finally left their location, Leora released a breath. It fogged the air in front of her face. *Please don't let them see it.*

Soon, the noise of tromping through underbrush faded. Was it safe to leave their hiding place?

"Should we leave?" Leora asked when Fletcher remained still.

"Yes, let's go. We have to get as far away from here as possible. They'll soon realize we didn't go the way they're headed." Fletcher struggled to stand and waited for Leora.

Molly held her position until Fletcher gave her the order to move.

"We can't go back to Ethan's house in case anyone is watching. Heading left will take us back to Sam's place. Looks like we go right. Come, Molly." The dog immediately heeded Fletcher's voice and left her resting place.

The shepherd sniffed the air and quickly picked up her trail again. Leora had to believe if Ethan and Tanner had been at Sam's and escaped, then Molly would be tracking Ethan's scent. It gave her hope. They had a chance at finding Ethan and Tanner first.

A determined Molly headed them deeper into

the wilderness. Once they'd covered enough space where they could no longer hear the men's voices, Fletcher slowed their speed.

"Maybe we should take a break?" he said to the sound of her labored breathing. "We're safe for the moment."

She shook her head. "We can't. Ethan and Tanner are out there somewhere. They could be hurt much worse than we are. I'm fine. I want to keep going."

"All right." Fletcher continued to keep watch on their surroundings as if expecting Sam and his crew to appear again.

Something caught Leora's attention up ahead mostly because Molly had zeroed in on a spot on the ground. She had something.

Please don't let it be Ethan or Tanner.

FOUR

Fletcher covered the space between him and the dog as quickly as possible while Leora followed.

"What do you have, girl?" Fletcher leaned past the dog to pick up what appeared to be a piece of material. He held it closer so he could see through the darkness.

"Is it Ethan's?"

"Possibly. Molly would certainly recognize Ethan's scent on it. But Ethan wouldn't have left it there deliberately. Chances are it got caught on the underbrush and he wasn't even aware of it." As a trained soldier, Ethan would know not to leave a visible trail behind with armed thugs scouring the woods. Fletcher didn't want to think about what these people would do to Ethan if they found him.

"He's still on the move," Leora concluded. "I sure hope Tanner is with him."

Fletcher held the scrap of fabric out to Molly to reinforce the scent. "Seek." She immediately stuck her nose to the ground, found the scent again, and bounded after it.

He and Leora began walking again.

"Molly responds well to you."

"She's a *gut* dog. Ethan told me Molly had been trained in numerous combat situations, including detecting and finding injured soldiers, and drug and explosive reconnaissance." He glanced her way. Like Ethan, the dogs had become Fletcher's passion.

Leora smiled. "Tanner mentioned Ethan had started training dogs after his last visit here."

Tanner had visited Ethan's ranch…

Fletcher nodded. "I didn't realize your *bruder* had been here before."

Leora frowned. "Really? He came here several months back…or at least I thought he and Ethan had met up here. Maybe I'm mistaken. I'm learning there are many things Tanner kept secret from me." She sighed. "So, you help Ethan train the dogs?"

He inclined his head. "*Jah*. It's been a rewarding endeavor. Ethan and I and my *bruder* Mason have been working together as hunting guides and helping out with the local search and rescue teams."

She turned her head his way. "That must be challenging."

"It is at times, but also very rewarding."

His *daed* and *grossdaddi* both had instilled in Fletcher and his brothers the desire to give back to the community they called home. For Fletcher, it was easy to do. He loved living in West Kootenai. Loved how close he was to his family and the *gut* friends he'd made through the years. He couldn't imagine living anywhere else.

At one time, he'd thought Catherine had felt the same way—they'd even planned the life they'd share here as youngsters. When she'd told him she wanted to leave West Kootenai, it had hit him like a physical blow. What Catherine had wished for had been worlds apart from what he'd imagined. In the end, he'd realized their differences were too great to overcome. There would be no future with Catherine.

He'd wallowed in the pain and the hole her severing their relationship had left in his heart to the point where he couldn't seem to dig himself out. When Ethan had asked him to help with the dogs' training, Fletcher had jumped at the chance, although he suspected Ethan had realized he needed a distraction from the hurt.

"It must be nice helping others so much," she said as they walked.

"It really is." Fletcher listened for any sounds they were being followed. In the distance, scraps of conversation drifted their way. He stopped for a moment. "They appear to be heading toward the road up ahead. They probably figure we'd try to reach it. For now, it's best if we keep going on this path."

She glanced around the soggy woods. "I sure hope we can find someplace with a phone soon. We need help. Sooner or later, they're going to find us." She shivered and gathered her cloak tighter.

"You're right. It's getting colder, and the rain isn't letting up." He glanced at the weeping skies peeking through the trees. Though Leora wore a cloak, it was soaked through. His coat wasn't much better, but at least it might be a bit warmer. Fletcher carefully shrugged out of it minding his injured shoulder. "Here, put this on."

"Oh, I couldn't. You need it."

He shook his head. "I'll be fine for a little while, and the coat is much heavier than your cloak." He placed it over her shoulders. Leora slipped her arms through while favoring her wrist.

"How're you holding up?" He pointed to her swollen wrist.

"It barely hurts." She dismissed his concern. "How bad is the ankle? It must be hard to keep putting pressure on it."

"To be honest, I'm not sure." He grimaced.

"First chance we get, I'll have a look. I know it's sprained, but I can't tell how badly." He didn't bring up his injured shoulder or the bump on the back of his head.

"Did your *bruder* mention having trouble with someone?" Fletcher was a person who saw the world logically, for the most part, and yet nothing about what had happened seemed logical.

"Now that you mention it, there was something Tanner said a few days before I lost contact with him. He'd stopped by my house. He was on his way to make a delivery, but it didn't have to be there for a few days." She noticed his confusion and said, "Tanner drives a truck for a delivery company transporting artwork around the northwest."

Though his family used wagons to deliver their furniture, Fletcher had seen many trucks delivering items to the places where they sold their pieces. He'd had occasion to speak with some of the drivers from time to time. Most were hardworking men and women. Many talked about the schedules they were forced to keep. At times, it could be difficult to make the deadlines. "What did your *bruder* say to you?"

She kept her attention on Molly. "Tanner stayed overnight with me, and he seemed unusually jumpy. When I got up the following morning, he was awake already and had made breakfast. He had told me the night before that he planned to stay a few days and maybe stop by to see the rest of the family. Only, he was ready to leave when I awoke."

Fletcher frowned. "Do you have any idea what changed his mind?"

"I'm not sure, but I think it had something to do with his phone. It kept beeping, as if someone were messaging him. My *Englisch* employer has a cell phone. She showed it to me one day. When she receives messages, there is a certain sound associated with it. She had the same beep as what Tanner received."

"Did you ask him about it?" Fletcher thought about the simple phone he carried for search and rescue. Occasionally, he'd receive a group text. Usually it consisted of some news important enough to notify each of the participants but not critical enough for a direct call.

"I did. He told me it was his work and his delivery date had been moved up." She glanced his way. "I don't think it was the truth."

"Why do you say that?" Fletcher wondered if Tanner had been keeping the truth from her because he didn't want to worry his sister.

"It was more in the way he acted. Before he left the house to get into his truck, Tanner checked out the window as if he were looking for something—or someone."

Against his will, a tremor of alarm slithered down Fletcher's spine. Had Tanner known the trouble coming after him and gone to Leora's home to hide out?

Leora sighed softly. "As he was leaving, he told me if anything were to happen to him, I should get in touch with Ethan. He would know what to do."

This had Fletcher's head swinging her way. "Did he say what might happen to him?"

She shook her head. "No, and he didn't really give me time to ask. He kissed me on my cheek and then left. That was the last I saw of my *bruder*."

As interesting as it was to guess what Tanner might have been hiding, it was really only speculation.

"I called Tanner later the same day and he answered. I asked him about what he'd said, and he brushed it off. Tanner told me he'd been under a lot of stress with his new route. He'd only recently started delivering artwork to different galleries around Colorado and surrounding states. I wanted to believe him." She shrugged.

"But you didn't."

"Not really. As I've said, Tanner and I are twins. We have a connection that is hard to describe. But he told me not to worry, and so I tried. When Tanner stopped returning my calls,

I called his employer who told me Tanner had texted him to say he was quitting."

Fletcher stopped walking. "You're kidding. When?"

"According to his employer, after he delivered his last load. He said Tanner had left his truck at the gallery. Nothing about what he said made sense. My *bruder* wouldn't act so irresponsibly. He loved his job and would never disappear and not get in touch with me. Even when he was traveling around after he got out of the service, Tanner always kept in touch. He'd find a way."

"Maybe someone else sent the text. Do you think that whoever was texting Tanner before the trip had something to do with his disappearance?"

Leora nodded. "There's no doubt in my mind. Tanner was worried about something. It turns out his fears were justified."

A sense of uneasiness returned. Fletcher looked over his shoulder before asking, "So, when you couldn't reach your brother, you called Ethan."

"Exactly. Ethan told me he'd go speak with Tanner's employer in person and see if he could get a better idea of what happened. I was so relieved. Tanner and I had lost so much already. I couldn't lose him, too."

Fletcher thought about his own family's history. His four *bruders* had had their share of troubles. Mason and Eli had been at odds with each other for years. Eli's first wife had been murdered. They had known their share of violence. He could certainly relate to what Leora and her *bruder* had gone through.

They started walking again. "Did you hear from Ethan after he spoke to Tanner's employer?"

She shook her head. "Ethan had told me when his meeting was with Zeke Bowman, the owner of Bowman Transportation, and he'd promised to call right after. Only, I never heard from him. When I couldn't reach Ethan after a few days, I came here."

And she and Fletcher had ended up at the wrong place at the wrong time and had both been thrown into a nightmare neither understood. His mind still couldn't take in everything they'd gone through or the reason behind it. Even after doing countless search and rescue missions, nothing about those had prepared him for this.

And they were still a long way from being safe. Every second they were out in the woods like this, they stood the risk of being recaptured.

"Do you mind if we stop for a second?" Leora's voice came out breathy. His attention went to her face, and the worry from earlier returned.

"Not at all." He found a lodgepole pine for them to take cover under. "At least it allows some shelter from the rain." Though the wind continued to chill. Fletcher knew only too well how dangerous long-term exposure to the elements could be.

"Denki." Leora took off his coat and handed it back to him. "I'm *oke* now," she assured him when he protested. "My cloak has dried some, and it's warm enough."

Fletcher struggled into the coat once more.

"You hurt your shoulder in the fall. How bad is it?"

"Not as bad as my ankle." He grinned and knelt to take a look. Getting the boot off was a struggle in itself. The ankle had swollen to almost double its normal size. "We'll need to wrap it tight, as well as your wrist, before we do any more damage."

Fletcher removed his knife and cut strips of the fleece lining from his coat to use as bandages. He worked to secure the ankle as tight as he could stand it. Once he'd finished, he forced his boot back on over the bandage and tested it out. "This feels better at least. Let me have a look at your wrist."

Leora held it out to him. Like his ankle, the wrist was badly swollen. He did his best to secure it without hurting her. It would have to do for now.

"As much as I wish we could rest longer, we don't have the luxury. It's best not to let Molly get too far ahead of us."

Though the dog was trained to bark should she find her target, the last thing they'd need was for Molly to give their location away. Especially if it meant they'd find a severely injured Ethan or worse.

They'd covered only a short space when he noticed the dog had stopped and was trained on something new.

"Oh, no." Fletcher hurried to the dog. Once he reached the spot, he struggled to see what Molly had found while praying it wasn't Ethan. "What is it, girl?"

The German shepherd glanced his way briefly before her attention went back to the ground. Fletcher leaned in closer. The rain had peppered the ground, but there was something on the grass. It grabbed his attention right away. A ruddy pool that looked out of place. Blood.

Please, Gott, *keep them both safe.*

Leora bent down and spotted what he had. "Is that blood? Oh, no… Ethan."

Fletcher straightened. "We don't know for certain it's Ethan's. It could belong to an animal."

"But if the dog picked it up…" Her gaze locked onto his. "Do you think they're dead?"

Fletcher couldn't let himself go there. "We can't jump to conclusions at this point. We have to keep searching for him. We'll find him and Tanner."

She slowly nodded. "You're right. Ethan and Tanner need us to be strong."

"Search, Molly." The dog reluctantly left the spot and soon was on the trail again. "She's found the scent again. A *gut* sign. It means Ethan is still free. Hopefully, your *bruder* is with him."

Or it could mean they'd both been captured and carried from the area by those men. *Don't go there…* Once more, Fletcher regretted not remembering his phone. Or alerting Aaron, or Eli, or Hunter—someone who would know to look for him should he not return. No one knew he was missing. He wondered about Leora.

"Did you tell anyone you were coming here?"

Leora appeared surprised by the question. "Why do you ask?" He told her his thoughts and she said, "Only my boss. I wanted her to know I had to take some personal time and would probably be gone for a week." That meant her boss wouldn't be looking for Leora for at least a week.

Molly continued to work her way through

the woods with the efficiency of a well-trained soldier.

With dark thoughts crowding in, Fletcher searched for something to take his mind off what they were facing. "How long has your *bruder* been out of the service?" he asked while keeping a close eye on their surroundings. After what they'd been through, letting down their guard wasn't an option.

He remembered Ethan telling him he'd been out of the service for more than five years.

"Only a couple of years. He stayed on after Ethan left the service, but things were different—I could hear it in his voice. Tanner told me he was scared the entire time he was in Afghanistan without Ethan. When his tour ended, he came back home to Colorado. I was so glad because I thought he was finally safe, and I guess I'd hoped he would stay." She shook her head. "But he didn't. There was a change in him. He'd become withdrawn. On edge. It seemed all the progress he'd made by being in Ethan's unit had been destroyed."

Fletcher thought about Mason. The rift between him and Eli had been hard on the family. Mason had left the faith and later joined the US Marshals. He remembered when his *bruder* had first come home, he'd been different. Mason had told him it was the things he'd seen while with the Marshals Service. Terrible things. Over time, Mason had slowly been returning to his old self, but watching his *bruder*'s struggles had served to affirm how much the community meant to Fletcher and why he never wanted to leave it.

"But when Tanner got this new job, he almost seemed like his old self. He was happy again."

"Until the last time he visited."

"*Jah*, until the last time." She grew silent. He could almost see the fear radiating from her.

A noise he couldn't identify grabbed his attention. His heart leaped to his throat as he jerked toward it. When he spotted a deer in the trees nearby, the relief was all-consuming.

He and his *bruders* had been hunting these woods since he'd been old enough to hunt. They'd become one of his favorite places. Always changing with the seasons, at times he felt more at ease in the wild like this than he did around others.

"How long was it after you last spoke to Tanner before those men showed up at your house?"

"A week maybe, but someone had been in my home before."

She had his full attention. "You're kidding. Did they take anything?"

She shook her head. "They tore the place up much like they had at Ethan's. And then someone called my work and demanded Tanner return what he'd taken."

Fletcher wondered if she was even aware of the way her voice shook as she recalled the incident.

"Then armed men broke in while I was at home and told me I had a day to return what Tanner stole, otherwise they'd come back and 'take care' of me like they would Tanner." She stopped walking and faced him. "I left. As soon as I was sure they were gone, I left. There was no way I could stay in my own home any longer. When I couldn't reach Ethan, I came here."

Up ahead, Molly kept up the vigilant search for her friend. Fletcher couldn't get the blood on the ground out of his head.

He was grateful for Molly's extensive military training that allowed her to point out blood as well as zero in on a scent. Did it belong to Ethan or Tanner? Fletcher still couldn't understand how their attackers had managed to get Ethan into custody.

"You said you thought those men had followed you here, but they were already at Ethan's. They'd searched the place and had taken Ethan and Tanner before you arrived. They somehow knew about his connection to Tanner. Maybe they were able to track him through Tanner's phone."

He could tell how difficult this was to believe. He'd once been as innocent. "Whatever is happening here isn't your fault. You mustn't take on their blame."

Fletcher couldn't explain this instant connection he felt to Leora. Perhaps it was the dangerous situation they'd been thrown in together. Life-and-death situations had a way of heightening emotions. Not that it mattered. His heart had been damaged beyond repair. He had nothing left to give anyone.

His mouth thinned when he thought about Catherine. He'd loved her so much. The pain of hearing her say she wanted to marry someone else still hurt.

From up ahead, Molly charged toward them, emitting a low, alarming growl.

"What is it, girl?" Fletcher asked and knelt beside the dog. But Molly wasn't looking at him. She was watching something behind them.

Fletcher quickly whirled around in time to see a flashlight coming up behind them. "Quick." He rose and grabbed Leora's arm. Together they ran through the damp woods while the dog kept protectively close. At this point, Fletcher had no idea where he was going, only that they had to get as far away from danger as possible.

"Over here. There's a footprint. Looks like they headed this way." It was Sam's voice.

"We'll never outrun them," Leora murmured.

Her frightened eyes confirmed she was counting on him to save them. Fletcher searched the darkness for some place to hide. There was no downed log this time. Only miles and miles of trees and no way to escape.

The world around her blurred. Leora tried to hold on, but she was all out of strength and fading fast.

"Fletcher." She grabbed his arm. "Help me."

Fletcher searched her face. "What's wrong?"

Getting the words out was impossible. He lifted her into his strong arms and ran. Leora couldn't imagine how hard it was for him to bear her weight on his injured ankle.

Leora rested her head against his shoulder while he hurried through the woods.

The men behind them were gaining.

Fletcher ran toward the dense foliage. "This will give us some cover at least." Yet if the men were following their footsteps, they'd be led right to them.

"We'd better find them soon," Sam's anxious voice pierced through to their hiding place. "It's bad enough the other two are still out there. You know what he's capable of doing to those who fail him."

Leora's gaze shot to Fletcher's. They still hadn't found Ethan and Tanner.

"If they keep coming this way, they're going to find us," Fletcher whispered close to her ear. "I'm going to try and draw their attention away from you." He set her on her feet, leaned down and gave Molly a command to stay.

"*Nay*, Fletcher." She grabbed his arm. "It's too dangerous."

He stopped and looked into her troubled eyes, and her chest tightened.

"I'll be fine. Stay here with Molly and try to be as quiet as possible."

With a final searching look, he headed off, away from her and the dog.

With him gone, Leora sank down beside the German shepherd and put her arm around the dog. Having another living thing close helped. Molly licked her cheek as if trying to comfort.

"Over there," a different man yelled. Shots rang out. Leora covered her mouth with her hand.

Gott, please keep him safe.

The noise of multiple footsteps running through the woods was terrifying, yet Leora didn't dare move. She couldn't imagine how hard it was for Molly to stay out of the action.

Soon, the footsteps faded, and her heartbeat returned to normal. Where was Fletcher?

Leora slowly rose and peeked around the tree. There was nothing but darkness and the rain. What should she do?

With one terrifying thought after another chasing through her mind, something shifted behind her. Molly charged toward it. Leora shrank against the tree.

"It's me, Molly."

Recognizing Fletcher's voice, Leora had never been happier to hear it. She ran to his side. "What happened? I heard shots."

"I'll tell you everything, but right now we have to keep moving." He reached for her arm to help her navigate the underbrush.

When they'd covered some distance, Fletcher stopped to look behind them. "I don't see anyone. I think we've lost them for now."

"Do you have any idea where we are?" The heavily treed woods all looked the same to her.

"I believe so. This is all still part of the Kootenai National Forest. Though with the rain and the dense woods, it's hard to get my bearings."

Her expression fell. "How do we find Ethan and Tanner and get out of here before they kill us?"

"The only way is for Molly to get back on Ethan's scent. But first, we need to let those men get farther ahead of us. If Ethan and Tanner are still on the move, then they may try to locate an *Englisch* house or find some other way to call the sheriff."

"Nothing about what's happening now makes sense. We need Ethan and Tanner to tell us what really happened." She shook her head. And they had to stay alive themselves. With so many men searching the woods for them, it wouldn't be easy.

Molly sniffed the air, as if searching for a scent.

"For the time being, let's keep going this way," Fletcher told her. "Hopefully, Molly can pick up Ethan's trail again. We'll skirt around the path those men took and hopefully be able to keep an eye out for them." He tucked her hand in his. "We'll find them. At least the rain appears to be letting up. That's something."

The endless walking was taking its toll on her depleted strength. "I know it hasn't been that long since we stopped, but do you mind if we take a moment to catch our breaths?"

Fletcher shook his head. "Over there. You can sit for a minute, and I'll take a look around with Molly."

She nodded and sank down to the damp log, grateful for a moment of a rest.

Clearly, Tanner didn't hide the stuff here.

The words of those intruders were all she'd thought about. What had Tanner gotten himself entangled in that had summoned these dangerous people to her door?

She and Tanner had always been so close. As twins, they could almost finish each other's thoughts. Leora experienced the same emotions Tanner went through. After he'd started working for the transportation company, he'd seemed happy, and it meant the world to Leora to have him finally smiling again.

For the longest time following their parents' deaths, she'd felt as if she'd lost him along with her parents. Even more so when Tanner joined the military. And, truthfully, even after he'd returned stateside. Leora rarely saw him, and she missed her *bruder*—wished they were closer, particularly after she'd received the cancer diagnoses. Yet at times it was as if she were all alone with no one to share her fears. Her great-aunt and -uncle weren't in the best of health. She couldn't burden them. Martha, her employer knew, but Leora would have loved to share her deepest concerns about dying with Tanner.

"I think it's safe to keep going. I don't see them anymore," Fletcher said, pulling her away from the troubled past.

Leora rose and brushed off her dress. "Then we should take advantage and keep going."

In the darkness, it was impossible to see beyond a few feet in front of them. It felt like they'd been walking for hours when Molly raced in the direction of what appeared to be a structure.

"What is that?" Leora squinted through the darkness to try to make it out.

"It looks like a shack. It was probably an old homesteader's place at one time."

Shelter to escape the cold and rain sounded wonderful right now. She started after the dog when Fletcher stopped her. "Hang on. We don't know what's inside."

Leora hadn't thought about what might be lurking within those crumbling walls.

As they neared, she could make out more. The place hadn't been inhabited in years and was slowly decaying to the ground. Her heart sank. At least they could get out of the weather for a bit.

The dog disappeared inside. Leora could hear Molly moving around the space.

"Stay behind me."

Leora nodded and slipped behind him as they entered the house. Pitch black greeted them. Leora glued herself to Fletcher's side as her eyes slowly adjusted to the darkness. Nothing but four walls barely hanging on.

"At least the roof appears intact." Fletcher glanced above them. "The rain can't get to us."

"Do you think we can stay for a bit to dry off?"

He faced her with a gentle smile. "For a bit. It's cold and we're both soaked. Why don't you sit for a little while? We'll rest and then head out."

Before Leora could sink to the dirt floor, the dog zeroed in on something near one corner.

"What is it, Molly?" Fletcher headed over to investigate. He knelt and picked up something from the floor.

Leora stepped closer to see. "Another swatch of cloth."

"It matches the earlier one. It looks as if it was ripped from the bottom of his shirt. Perhaps Ethan used it as a makeshift bandage. At least we know he's been here at one time." Fletcher held the cloth close to get a better look. "The material is flannel like some of the ones I've seen Ethan wear before." He peered out the window. "It's been a while since my *bruders* and I came this way, but if I remember correctly, there's a fairly large *Englisch* logging business that operates out of the area. It's on private land bordering the wilderness. They have a huge storage facility on sight as well as an office. There's a phone. I remember seeing it when I went there once. Ethan would know this. If he was able to escape, he'd go there."

She squeezed his arm. "That's *gut* to hear." Reaching the logging company was their best chance of getting help. She prayed once they found it, Ethan and Tanner would be there, as well.

An empty window frame where glass had once been blew cold air into the space. "Do you think they will know about the logging business?"

Fletcher shook his head. "I sure hope not."

Leora desperately wanted to believe they'd find Ethan and her *bruder* soon.

"Ethan is a former soldier, and he knows this area like the back of his hand. So is your brother. They can take care of themselves."

The image of the blood they'd seen on the door and in the woods came to mind. "But one of them is hurt."

Fletcher glanced down to the cloth in his hand. "Still, it appears Ethan is able to keep moving. He's strong. He told me many times about the injuries he sustained while in combat. He's tough. If Tanner is with him, they've both been in far worse situations. They're far better equipped to handle whatever this is than we are."

She let out a sigh. "You're right."

"Let me take a look at your wrist, and then I'll rebandage it and my ankle before we head out."

He flexed his shoulder and winced. "Just a little tender," he said to her worried look. Fletcher carefully unwrapped the bandage from her wrist and examined it as gently as possible. "It doesn't appear to be any worse for wear." He replaced the bandage.

"Let me help you with your ankle. After putting pressure on it for so long, it's bound to be swollen." Leora waited for him to sink to the floor.

He tried to get the boot off by himself but couldn't.

Leora grabbed hold of it and pulled hard. Fletcher let out a low groan when the boot slipped past his injured ankle.

"Sorry about that." She sat the boot aside and gently removed the dressing. There was no mistaking that the ankle was in far worse shape than before. "Oh, Fletcher, this isn't *gut*." She glanced up and saw him fighting back pain.

"It'll be *oke*. Wrap it up as tight as you can to keep it stable. We don't have a choice. Every second we're sitting still, we run the risk of being captured." He held her gaze. "We can't let that happen."

She couldn't imagine how he managed walking when every step had to be excruciating.

"This may hurt," she told him and bit her bottom lip as she secured the ankle as tightly as she could get it while Fletcher closed his eyes, his jaw clamped tight.

Once she'd finished, Leora helped him get the boot back on.

Fletcher rose and put pressure on the injury. "*Denki*. This feels much better. We can stay here a few more minutes," he said, as if seeing the exhaustion she couldn't begin to hide.

It wasn't lost on Leora the danger they faced by remaining still for too long.

She slowly lowered herself to the dusty floor and leaned against the wall, grateful for a chance to rest. Her body ached all over. Her strength was almost nonexistent.

Outside, the wind blew through the empty window frame with renewed fury, sending rain scattering across the room. But there was something more than the cold and the rain. It grabbed her attention right away.

Someone was out there.

FIVE

Molly growled low while the hackles on her back rose. She would defend them to the death, but they couldn't afford to get into a confrontation here in the small confines of this house.

Fletcher stumbled to his feet and pulled Leora up beside him. "We've got to get out of here. There's no place to hide where they won't see us."

Keeping her close, Fletcher headed for the door, grateful they'd left it open. The noise it had made when they came in had been loud.

Molly slipped outside. Once he and Leora followed, Fletcher pointed to the side of the house. If they could make it there and get out of sight, they stood a chance at escaping.

Fletcher clutched Leora's hand and pulled her along with him while glancing over his shoulder to gauge their pursuers' location. Flashlights appeared near the opposite side of the structure.

Fletcher put himself between Leora and the danger while Molly was on high alert.

"Check inside. There are footprints all around this place. They could be hiding in there," Sam ordered. He appeared to be calling the shots now. They hadn't seen Jade in quite some time.

Multiple footsteps descended on the house. Staying here was no longer an option.

"It won't take them long to realize we're not inside." Fletcher slowly leaned forward enough to see what was happening near the entrance. Several men stood close to the door. Fletcher quickly ducked out of sight.

"Sam, are you there?" A man's voice came through a walkie-talkie the men were using to communicate.

"Yeah, I'm here. What's up? We believe we're close to finding Tanner's sister and the Amish man with her." There was irritation in Sam's tone, almost as if he resented being interrupted.

"Well, Jade believes she is zeroing in on Tanner's location. She doesn't think Connors is with him, though. Somehow he and Tanner got separated. Keep watch for him, as well. He's hurt. It should slow him down."

"Fine. We'll keep after the sister and hopefully Connors. They can't hide forever. We'll find them," Sam assured the man.

"You'd better. We have to get this thing contained before one of them escapes the woods and reaches law enforcement. That can't happen."

Sam grumbled something Fletcher couldn't hear.

Stunned, Fletcher tried to make sense of what they'd learned. Tanner and Ethan had gotten separated. Jade's people were closing in on Tanner. If they captured him, Fletcher had no idea how he and Leora would be able to free him.

"I heard a sound over by the side of the house," someone said, pulling Fletcher's attention away from his troubled thoughts.

"Well, what are you waiting for? Go check it out," Sam barked.

Fletcher and Leora were all out of time. He grabbed her hand and ran through the woods, Molly leading the way. They couldn't fight all those men. Getting away was their only chance at survival.

Fletcher tried to ignore the pain in his ankle, but it reminded him with each step he was at a disadvantage.

"Over there. I see them." They'd been spotted.

"Hurry, Leora."

A gunshot cracked through the woods. The men were shooting at them.

"Get down." The words had barely crossed his lips when another round flew through the trees.

He and Leora ducked low and kept going.

"I can't believe this is happening," Leora exclaimed in disbelief. These guys were ruthless, and they were worried about whatever Tanner had taken falling into the wrong hands.

"Stop your shooting. We need her alive," Sam yelled. "Don't let them get away."

Flashlights beamed all around them. At least by staying low, they were able to dodge the lights, but they couldn't outrun these shooters for long.

Gott, we need Your guidance.

The group was closing in.

Help me!

Over his and Leora's labored breathing came a welcomed sound. Running water off to his left. A stream was nearby. If they could get out of sight for the moment, the water would help to hide their footprints.

Fletcher slipped his hand into Leora's and ran. They were almost right on top of the stream before he spotted it.

"If we can find a place to get out of sight, they might pass us by." He looked around the darkness. As much as he hated going into the water considering the cold, it would work to their benefit.

He held on to Leora's hand as they stepped into the water. Fletcher almost tripped over a tree that had fallen into the stream.

"Let's crouch down low on the other side of this. If they pass by, they'll think we headed downstream." At least this was the hope. He prayed it would work.

Fletcher climbed over the log and then helped Leora across.

"Stay close, Molly." The dog obeyed and jumped over the tree.

They squatted together, hidden by the log. The ice-cold water seeped through his boots and up his trouser legs.

Fletcher pulled Leora into his arms. He could feel her shivering, probably more from fear than the penetrating cold.

Several tense moments later, the flashlights appeared. His heart sank. Leora spotted them, as well, and buried her face against his chest.

"Any sign of them?" Sam's anxious voice sounded almost right on top of where they hid. The lights scanned the area, coming so close Fletcher was sure they'd be spotted.

"Their footprints head into the stream," a man said. "I'm guessing they're using it to keep their direction hidden."

"I'm not going into the water. I'll radio the others. They can meet us upstream. Let's go." Sam didn't want to get wet, which would work in their favor.

The men kept to the shore while searching the underbrush around the stream.

Fletcher stayed low, his hand on the dog. Molly wasn't one for sitting still with danger close.

"I don't see any footprints on the shore." Sam again. "They're definitely using the water to disguise their movement."

Soon, the noise grew faint. Fletcher lifted his head and strained to see the flashlights. "It looks like they bought our diversion for the moment. Once their people arrive at the end of the stream, they'll know we didn't go that way and they'll circle back around. Let's see if we can find the logging business and call for help."

With another careful look around, Fletcher rose. He climbed up the slippery bank and held out his hand to assist Leora.

"Which way is it from here?" Leora asked over her chattering teeth.

Fletcher took a second to find his direction. "This way, I think." As they walked, he looked for anything to confirm he and Leora were on the right track. In recent years, he'd done plenty of searches in these very woods but never under these circumstances. Fleeing for your life made it easy to get turned around. With the rain and the darkness as added deterrents, there weren't any natural milestones visible to confirm this was the right direction. Simply Fletcher drawing from his past memories.

The need to keep a fast pace was difficult with his ankle giving him grief. If he remembered correctly, the stream wasn't very big. It wouldn't take Sam's people long to figure out they'd been fooled.

Leora kept glancing behind them. "I don't see them back there so far."

Fletcher hoped they could put enough space between them and their trackers to reach the logging business.

The last time he'd been there with his *bruders*, Fletcher had been impressed by the sheer magnitude of what they'd been able to process each day. The office had been humming with activity, the receptionist stationed in front answering phone calls.

Molly continuously sniffed the air to locate Ethan's scent while Fletcher tried not to lose hope. If Ethan hadn't come this way, then where was he? How had he and Tanner gotten separated?

Leora stumbled over something on the ground. Fletcher caught her before she could fall.

"*Denki*," she murmured in a thready voice. The pallor of her complexion and the labored breathing spoke of something far more severe than simply physical exhaustion.

Both of his boots were filled with water. "Let's stop long enough to dump the water out of our shoes." He found a tree trunk and sat. Pulling his boot off over the swollen ankle wasn't easy.

"I've got it." Leora grabbed the boot and tugged until it freed. Water poured out of it. His socks were dripping wet. He removed them and rang out the water while Leora did the same.

"How are you holding up?" he asked as he carefully replaced his sock. She was young and yet she appeared to be struggling physically. Fletcher didn't believe her condition was simply related to exhaustion from the trip from Colorado. She didn't trust him with the truth yet.

"Wet, but thankful to be alive after what happened back there."

He smiled at the way she tried to put a positive spin on what had happened. "I guess it could be far worse." Thanks to Leora's bandaging skills, his ankle hadn't suffered any further damage. But he wasn't foolish enough to think they could keep running forever. If they could reach the logging business and call for help, his friend Sheriff Collins would dispatch deputies to bring them in. Once they were safe, hopefully, with the sheriff's help, they'd be able to find out where Ethan and Tanner were.

"Shall we keep going?" Leora asked. He admired her courage.

"*Jah*, let's keep moving." As they walked, Fletcher listened to faint voices coming from near the stream. The flashlights were still some distance back. He blew out a relieved sigh. At least they had some breathing room.

Leora had noticed him looking over his shoulder and did the same.

"It's safe for now," he assured her. "But we need to get to the logging business soon." There were at least two different groups of men searching for them as well as Ethan. Another group was closing in on Tanner. There could be more. This was way beyond what he was capable of figuring out.

Fletcher tried to determine the time. When he'd gone to Ethan's, it had been late afternoon. It was probably early morning, which meant they'd have hours to survive before daylight, and it was impossible to see anything. At any moment they could be walking into a trap.

She didn't want to think about what might happen to her *bruder* if he were captured. Though she had her great-aunt and -uncle, they weren't very close. She and Tanner had always looked out for each other.

"Did Tanner live close to your community

when he wasn't on the road?" Fletcher was trying to make sense of things by asking questions. She understood.

"*Nay.* He lives closer to the company's headquarters in Denver. I wanted him to stay with me in our grandparents' old house. Both have passed away, and it's only me there. Our aunt and uncle still live in the community, though they are a little way from my house."

Leora believed for Tanner, being back among the Amish ways served as a painful reminder of the life he'd once loved and what they'd both lost. Once more, the guilt she'd carried with her since their parents' death returned. She'd behaved so recklessly during her *Rumspringa.* Attending *Englischer* parties all the time with people she barely knew. Taking rides with strangers to other neighboring towns without telling her parents. Staying out all hours of the night. Leora had never gotten the chance to apologize to her parents for the worry she'd caused. Because of her wild adolescence, she and Tanner had grown apart during their *Rumspringa.* Their relationship had never really recovered.

"Did Tanner have any problems with his job— Sorry," he said when she frowned. "I'm looking for answers."

Leora nodded. "It's *oke.* I've been running everything over in my head looking for answers, as well. Tanner never mentioned having trouble. He appeared to love his job." She stopped suddenly. "I can't believe I almost forgot..."

"What?" Fletcher's full attention was on her face.

"Something which happened during his last visit. Tanner disappeared for several hours the afternoon before he left. When he returned, I asked him where he'd been. He told me he'd gone to visit family, but it wasn't true. Our aunt and uncle hadn't seen him in weeks."

Those men who'd broke into her house had accused Tanner of taking something that belonged to them. Was it possible Tanner had actually done as they'd claimed and hidden whatever it was somewhere near her home? What was so important they'd go to such extremes to get it back? Without more to go on, they might never figure it out. They needed to find Ethan and, hopefully, he would know where Tanner might have gotten separated.

"You said your parents died in a fire. Could this have something to do with that?"

Leora flinched at the mention of her parents' deaths. "I don't see how," she said at last. Whenever she thought about the time, she remembered her behavior. She cleared her throat. "It's been years since they died, and the person responsible for their deaths passed away in prison."

"Did you know the accused?" he asked curiously.

They had. "*Jah.* He was our *Englisch* neighbor and a police officer. Our parents were friends with him, and Tanner and I played with his daughters all the time. It never made sense. He was always so kind, and his daughters adored him. But the police and the fire investigators found the evidence they needed to convict him on multiple counts of arson and homicide.

"A gas can that had belonged to our neighbor was found near our family's destroyed home. Even though they couldn't prove he'd known there were people inside the house when the fire started, he was charged with a first-degree felony and sentenced to fifty years in prison. He died there a few years later."

"So this wasn't an isolated incident?"

"It was not. There were other fires but no other deaths." She was silent for a moment. "Still, I don't see how anything back then can be connected to what's going on now. Tanner and I went to live with our grandparents in Colorado soon after the fire. We've never gone back to our former home, though at some point I want to," she said with conviction. "I guess I think if I return there, maybe I can make peace with what happened." And maybe she could learn to forgive herself. Leora prayed that day would come, but she'd carried the guilt with her for so long. Every time she thought about the night of the fire and the argument she and Tanner had, the guilt threatened to swallow her up.

Tanner had promised to accompany her to a party but then changed his mind and tried to talk Leora out of going. She hadn't listened, and Tanner had gone looking for her later that evening, around the same time the fire occurred. She often wondered, but couldn't bring herself to ask, if he blamed her for their deaths. If he'd been home, perhaps he could have saved their parents. Or perhaps she would have lost him, too.

"I can understand." He told her about his *bruder* Eli. "The fire that had taken his first wife's life was emotionally devastating but knowing that the people around him believed he was actually the one responsible for setting the fire hurt terribly. Eli never wanted to return to Libby after he left. It was too hard. What about Tanner? Did he ever talk about going back?"

"Not really. Tanner took *Daed*'s death especially hard because they were so close."

She could see her answer was disappointing. Leora didn't believe their past had anything to do with what was taking place now.

With her body suffering from extreme exhaustion, not to mention the cold that seemed to slow every step, thinking clearly was difficult. Even if all the answers were right in front of her, Leora doubted if she could figure it out.

"Why had you gone to Ethan's house?" Leora asked him. They'd been so busy trying to stay alive that she hadn't thought to ask before now.

Fletcher told her about his last conversation with Ethan. "He's not usually so vague about his comings and goings. We've actually become quite close over time, which was why I thought it strange. I could tell this was something he didn't want to share for some reason."

He'd been worried about Tanner.

"Anyway, Ethan rarely goes more than a few days without reaching out to either myself or Mason. Since Mason is out of town and Ethan knew this, he would check in to see what was on our agenda. It's getting into hunting season, and there have been a few rescue missions already. He wouldn't not reach out. When I heard the shots, I couldn't shake the feeling something wasn't right."

It seemed they'd both been too late to help their friend. "If only I'd gotten there sooner. I might have been able to save Ethan."

"Or you could have ended up hurt or more likely taken."

The need for answers continued to grow stronger. Ethan, clearly injured, could be bleeding out somewhere. The man who had radioed Sam had said they were closing in on Tanner. They might have him by now. "When I called Ethan to tell him I hadn't heard from Tanner in a week, Ethan was instantly worried. That's when I knew this wasn't me overreacting."

Her answer clearly troubled Fletcher. "What do you mean?"

"Tanner kept in touch with Ethan, as well. When Ethan found out Tanner had left his truck unattended and simply vanished, and that his employer told me Tanner had quit, we both knew this wasn't like Tanner. At the time, I didn't realize Ethan still had Tanner's old number."

"His old number?"

"Tanner said he'd lost his old phone. He'd gotten a different one with a new number." She hesitated. "But the strange part is, this is the third time he's lost his phone recently."

Looking back at the incident and everything that had happened, Leora wondered if Tanner had been trying to stay hidden from the men coming after them now.

"Maybe Tanner was forced to abandon his truck because he was running from these dangerous men."

She'd thought the same thing. "Probably. I

was surprised Tanner hadn't reached out to Ethan, considering he was obviously in trouble."

"I think if he could, he would have. Until we find Ethan and Tanner and get answers, we're playing a guessing game. I say let's stay focused on reaching the building." He looked her way. "It's freezing, I know. Unfortunately, we can't do much about it, but if you need a break…"

She shook her head. "I'll be fine. I just want to get to them as soon as possible." They believed Molly had been focused on Ethan's scent for a while. She prayed Tanner was still with him and they hadn't gotten separated somehow.

Up ahead, Molly had zeroed in on something. A second later, she dashed through the woods.

"She's on the scent again," Fletcher told her with relief in his voice.

Trying to keep up with the determined Molly was hard, especially with both of them injured.

Occasionally the shepherd would stop and sniff the air to home in on the scent.

Leora had a feeling that whatever Molly found at the end of the trail would only be the beginning.

The thought had barely cleared her head when the ground beneath them began to give way.

"Leora!" Fletcher shouted, reaching for her. His fingers brushed hers, but it wasn't enough to hold on.

"Fletcher. Help me! I'm falling." She screamed. He tried to grab her wrist but couldn't.

Leora hit the ground hard. The wind left her body. She'd landed in a four-by-four-foot hole. It was deep—well over her head. She gasped in air and stared in horror as the soggy earth above her sloughed away, raining down mud everywhere. Leora scrambled to her feet and as far away from the mudslide as she could manage.

"Fletcher." She frantically searched the darkness above.

His face appeared. A relieved breath shuddered through her body.

"Are you hurt?" he asked then looked down at the ground.

"I'm *oke*." But her shaky voice revealed it wasn't true.

"Hang on. I'm going to look for a way to get you out of there."

He backed up as the earth under him continued to slide. "The ground is still collapsing."

Leora's frantic gaze searched the small space, which was filling with mud at an alarming rate. All she could think about was that she didn't want to die here.

Fletcher circled the gaping hole. "I'm going to grab a tree branch so I can pull you out. I'll be right back."

Molly peeked her head over the side. The dog was a welcomed sight. Molly held her position.

Leora tried to keep a positive outlook, but there was no way their pursuers wouldn't have heard the earth's rumblings, not to mention her screams. Time was running out.

The ground continued to collapse. The tiny space felt like a coffin.

"Grab hold of this." Fletcher lowered the lodgepole pine branch down to where she could reach it as his attention jerked toward something else. "Hurry, Leora. I see flashlights heading this way."

Her heart clenched, and she latched onto the branch. "I've got it."

"Hold on tight. I'm going to pull you up."

She kept her eyes fixed on Fletcher and prayed she would make it out in time.

He slowly pulled her up. Halfway to the surface, the branch cracked. Leora bit back a scream. This couldn't be happening.

"It's breaking," she said in an unsteady voice.

"Grab hold of it higher up."

Leora didn't want to let go.

"Quickly, Leora."

Leora stretched out her right hand as high as she could. She grabbed a handful of pine needles. The branch felt much thicker there. She repositioned her left hand up above the right.

Behind her, a terrifying sound had Leora jerking her head around. The ground continued to cave in. Fletcher quickly pulled her the rest of the way.

Leora still held on to the branch with a death grip. Fletcher grabbed her around the waist and helped her to her feet and into his arms. "I was so worried." He held her close, and slowly her heartbeat returned to normal.

The ground beneath was still falling away.

"The rest of this space is going into the hole. Let's get out of here." With his arm around Leora's waist, he called the dog to follow. They reached the woods. Behind them, multiple footsteps were getting closer.

"The sinkhole might work to our advantage," Fletcher told her. "It appears to be closing in on itself. Hopefully, they'll think it caved in on top of us. Unfortunately, I don't think they'll leave without having proof we're dead."

If Fletcher hadn't acted so quickly, Leora had little doubt she would have ended up buried beneath all that mud.

SIX

Fletcher stopped once they'd put some space between themselves and the sinkhole. "Take a moment to catch your breath. Are you hurt?"

"*Nay*, but I'm still shaking. It was so scary. I thought I would die."

Fletcher had been terrified he wouldn't be able to get her in time. His reaction to believing she might die scared him. He barely knew Leora. Sure, he cared for her as one human being to another, but...

His fingers shook as he brushed strands of her red hair from her face, his hand lingering on her cheek. Her huge eyes found him. Feelings he'd thought had died with Catherine returned.

Too soon, his head warned. Catherine's rejection still tasted bitter on his lips. *I want a* mann *who doesn't insist on remaining in West Kootenai forever.* Catherine wanted to travel; she'd longed for a warmer climate. But how could he leave the only place he'd ever called home, or the family who had been there for Fletcher his entire life?

In the end, Catherine had chosen another man. They planned to wed. She'd told Fletcher recently they would leave for Virginia soon after. Catherine hadn't even waited a year after she'd broken up with him to plan her wedding.

Fletcher had tried to forgive her for breaking his heart, yet seeing her at the biweekly church service had become like a knife to his heart. Many times, Fletcher had talked himself out of attending because of it.

"You're shivering." His voice came out rougher than intended. The way Leora reminded him of what once he'd longed for was hard to ignore. He removed his coat. "It's not dry, but it will help you warm up."

She didn't protest as he slipped it on.

"How are you doing?" she asked.

He couldn't deny having to use his injured shoulder to pull her out of the hole hadn't done it any favors.

"I'm going to take a closer look and see if those men are convinced we are buried under the mountain of mud." He gave the order for Molly to stay.

The shepherd responded as she'd been trained to do. Molly was a fine example of what he hoped to accomplish with the rest of the dogs in training someday. If they survived.

Fletcher studied Leora for a moment before heading back the way they'd come. She'd been through so much. All he wanted to do was to keep her safe and to find Ethan and Tanner. Hopefully, give her the answers she needed to put this terrible experience behind.

He did his best to keep the noise to a minimum as he retraced their steps. The sinkhole had been an unexpected shock. Of all the things they'd gone through, having the earth fall away from beneath them was the last thing he'd expected.

Fletcher had no idea what might have caused it. He'd read about such things in the past. Sinkholes mostly happened where the rock below the surface was limestone or carbonate. Sometimes they were attributed to rocks naturally dissolved by the groundwater circulating through them. As the rock softened, spaces and caverns developed underground. The recent rain plaguing the countryside had probably compromised the ground above the underground cavern, and their weight had been the last straw.

As he neared the spot, Fletcher noticed several flashlights closing in. He ducked behind a tree and strained to hear what they said.

Scraps of conversation drifted his way.

Fletcher peeked around the tree. The men believed he and Leora had gone into the sinkhole. One of the flashlight beams flashed across the space where the hole had once been. It was now covered by earth. If Fletcher had been a little slower in getting Leora out…

"He'll want proof. We can't take the chance they've somehow gotten away." This was Jade speaking. She was telling the men to dig up the hole to make sure.

"Aw, Jade, it'll take hours."

"I don't care. Do it. You—take some men and spread out to the right. See if you can find any trace of them. I'll check straight ahead."

"You want me to come with you, Jade? There's a lot of space to check."

"No, I don't need you to come with me. Get some shovels and start digging."

The woman obviously didn't like having her orders questioned.

Fletcher ducked back when she stepped his way. He'd waited too late to leave. There would be no way to escape without her seeing him. He flattened himself against the tree and watched the light grow closer. When it was almost right on top of him, the beam suddenly stopped moving. He held his breath and prayed desperately.

Jade had to be standing just on the other side of the tree. From where he stood, he could see his and Leora's footsteps. A second later, Jade started back toward the sinkhole.

Why wouldn't she keep pursuing him?

He quietly released the breath he'd held inside and eased far enough around to see that she'd reached her people.

"They didn't go that way."

Fletcher kept watching as the other search party returned. "There's no sign of them."

Jade ordered the men who were digging to stop. "There's only one place they can be and it's in the hole. Besides, we have bigger problems. Our people lost Tanner, and Connors is still out there somewhere. We can't let them reach the police. Come on. Let's head out."

Jade started off in the direction she and her men had come while Fletcher wondered if she'd actually missed their footprints. He didn't see how.

Fletcher moved to the other side of the tree and leaned down to see their footprints clearly visible.

"Gotcha."

Fletcher whirled toward the sound of the voice.

The person no longer wore his disguise as he aimed a gun at Fletcher. "Jade was wrong—I knew it. You were hiding right in front of her all along. She's not up to the task he's given her." He glanced past Fletcher. "Where's the sister?"

Fletcher wasn't about to give Leora up. "I don't know. We got separated."

The man smiled smugly. "Nice try. You're lying. She's with you. Let's go. I'm taking you both in. I can't wait to show *him* how incompetent Jade really is. By capturing you, he'll promote me over her."

When Fletcher didn't budge, the man shoved him hard. "I said let's go. Where's she hiding? Once I get you both, this will look good for me. I'll be the person who saved the day—not Jade."

Fletcher's mind worked overtime to come up with a plan of escape. Without a doubt, he would have no choice but to try to disarm the man as quickly as possible. His *bruders* had told him stories about how they'd been forced to go against the things they believed to save someone they loved. Love. The word stuck in his head. He didn't love Leora—love didn't work so quickly. It took time to cultivate—years even.

He couldn't deny that he felt a fierce duty to protect her. No matter what, he wouldn't lead this dangerous man to Leora. "She's this way." He pointed to the right.

The man scowled. "I don't believe you. The footprints say you went straight. You better not be trying to fool me. You'll regret it."

"We circled around to throw you off our

tracks," Fletcher told the man and held his gaze without flinching.

"All right, go." He shoved Fletcher hard. Fletcher stumbled but caught himself before he went sprawling on the wet ground. His captor fell in behind him while keeping the gun against his back as a reminder he meant business. At some point, Jade would notice this guy was missing and come looking. Fletcher didn't have long.

What would Ethan do in this situation? Ethan was one of the bravest men Fletcher knew. He'd keep fighting till his last breath.

Fletcher kept walking while looking for the right distraction to overpower the man as each step took him farther away from Leora.

The faintest of movement appeared off to his right side. A flash of blue. Leora. Fletcher tried not to draw attention to her. He wanted to warn her to go back before the man found her and they were both captured. He had to do something fast.

Fletcher stopped and focused on the ground. Jade and her people had left footprints. He pretended to study them.

"What's going on? Why are you stopping?" The man circled around to face Fletcher while pointing the gun in his face. "What kind of game are you playing?"

Fletcher thought fast. "I think she's on the run."

His captor's eyes narrowed. "Enough. What do you take me for?"

Fletcher looked past the man's shoulder. Leora had come closer. She held a log in her hand. Molly was at her side and ready to go into battle.

"Get moving." The man grabbed Fletcher by his collar. This was the moment Fletcher had been waiting for. He clasped the weapon, his action taking the man by surprise.

The gun went off, barely missing Fletcher. The shot would have alerted Jade and the others.

"Go, Molly!" Fletcher commanded. He could use the canine soldier's help right now because this guy was much stronger than he'd imagined, and Fletcher was injured.

They fought for control of the weapon. Fletcher could feel himself fading. Molly latched onto the man's leg. He yelped in pain and loosened his hold on the gun. And not a second too soon.

Fletcher managed to take possession of the weapon while the man continued to try to fend off Molly's attack.

Leora reached them. Wielding the log above her head, she smashed it against the man's head. He didn't have time to react. The blow knocked him out cold.

Molly released her grip.

Fletcher knelt and searched the guy's pockets, finding a flashlight but no phone. He grabbed the light. "They'll have heard the shot and investigate." Working quickly, Fletcher ripped out strips of his jacket lining to use as makeshift restraints as well as a gag. "That will keep him quiet." He rose and patted the dog's head. "Good job, Molly." The dog had his back. He turned to Leora. "Thank you for saving my life."

Together, they ran in the direction they'd originally been heading. The darkness of the woods closed in around them, making it next to impossible to see anything. They had no idea how long it had been since Ethan had come this way. What if they'd been following a trail that would lead them straight into their enemy's arms?

Flashlights dotted the darkness behind them. "They're coming."

Fletcher looked over his shoulder. "They've reached their person by now." His troubled gaze shifted to hers. "We can't slow down."

She understood this yet her broken body craved rest. Leora had been diagnosed with breast cancer for a second time a little over six months ago. Her doctor had wanted to start chemo treatments right after her surgery. He'd scheduled two weeks of treatment followed by a week of rest. Though Leora hadn't experienced hair loss, she'd suffered weight loss, nausea, and extreme fatigue. Her last treatment had ended a few days before she'd started this trip.

"I will be your strength," he told her, as if sensing she was in trouble. "Lean on me."

Leora caught her breath as she looked at the man who hadn't once hesitated to risk his life to save hers. Her first reaction had been right. Fletcher was a *gut* man.

He wrapped his arm around her waist and tugged her close. Among the unending danger facing them, feelings she thought she'd buried reminded her she was still alive.

After the death of her parents, then losing Tanner, Leora had learned to keep her emotional distance from others. What if she let someone into her heart and lost them, too? How could she bear that much pain again? With the added burden of battling cancer twice now, it had confirmed for Leora that she couldn't willingly cause the kind of pain for someone else, either.

She shook her head. It was simply emotions boiling up from what she'd gone through. She and Fletcher had been thrown together against insurmountable odds. It was bound to form bonds. If they survived this, she would return to Colorado. His life was here in West Kootenai. Their futures were not meant to be together.

"Jade was there at the sinkhole." He told her about the earth collapsing into the hole, covering it from view.

Leora pulled her thoughts back to the moment. "Did they believe we were in it when it collapsed?"

Fletcher shook his head. "I don't think so, but something strange happened." He told her how Jade had called off the hunt. "There is no way she couldn't have seen our footprints. I don't know what she's up to. There is more going on here than we realize." He looked behind them once more. "Helping their man will slow them down a bit."

But not for long.

Leora thought about what Fletcher had said about Jade. Why would Jade call off the search for them and then tell her men they'd probably perished in the collapse?

"I wish I understood anything about what's happening." She brushed back her wilting bonnet only to have it flop back onto her face. "Ugh." Leora removed the bonnet and then realized her prayer *kapp* was probably acting like a beacon to those searching for them. She took it off and left her hair uncovered. Not something she would normally do, but this wasn't normal.

"My apron." It would call attention. She

stopped walking and took it off, as well. Now what? She couldn't leave it here to be found.

"Put them in my coat pocket." Fletcher took the apron from her. The plastic baggy she'd forgotten about fell to the ground. It contained the vitamin supplements her doctor had recommended she take.

Fletcher picked it up, his attention on her face as he handed them back to her.

"Vitamins," she said without looking at him. She couldn't tell him the truth and have him look at her the way everyone else did when they found out she was a cancer survivor.

"We'll put them in the other pocket so you know where they are should you need them."

She was grateful he didn't question her further. "Here, you should take the coat back. My cloak is dry, thanks to this." Leora removed the garment and handed it to him. "You must be freezing by now."

He tried to refuse but she wouldn't let him. Eventually, Fletcher slipped into the coat. She didn't miss the way he flinched when he placed his injured arm into the sleeve.

"How is your shoulder and ankle after having to fight?"

Fletcher downplayed the injuries. "No worse for wear, I guess." Molly caught his attention, and Leora was able to watch him unnoticed for a moment. His hair touched the collar of his coat. Fletcher was a good six inches taller than she was. Broad shoulders confirmed what she knew to be true. He was a strong man with the heart of a protector.

Unexpectedly, his piercing green eyes found hers, taking her breath away.

Lean on me.

She hated being a prisoner to the disease, but right now—under these horrific circumstances—she needed his strength more than ever.

They continued moving through the woods, following Molly on her mission to find her owner.

Fletcher glanced behind them and frowned. In the predawn darkness, seeing anyone until they were right on top of them would be impossible. "I hear something. They're coming this way now. I hope we reach the logging business soon. We can't keep running through the woods like this. Eventually, they're going to catch up with us."

The odds were against them staying hidden, and they were greatly outnumbered.

Molly stopped suddenly, alerting them to something on the ground.

Leora and Fletcher hurried to the dog's side.

"A pen." Fletcher picked it up. "I recognize it. This is like the one Ethan had. Good girl,

Molly. Seek." The dog really didn't have to be told the command; she was anxious to get back on the trail. Almost as if she, too, realized the seriousness of their situation.

Fletcher stopped for a moment to study the path in front of them and knelt down. Leora looked over his shoulder. "What are you looking for?"

He pointed to the ground. There, along with Molly's paw prints, was a single set of shoe impressions. "I don't see any other human footprints. This has to be Ethan's, and it doesn't look as if anyone has been tracking him." He rose beside her. Fletcher looked around as if gaining his bearings. "I believe we're very close to the logging business."

At this time in the early morning, the business would be closed, but hopefully they could find a way in to use the landline and call for help.

Fletcher tucked the pen into his pocket, and they kept going.

Leora's attention returned to the lights behind them. "Oh, Fletcher, I think they're gaining on us." Suddenly, the flashlights vanished. "What's happening?"

"They're trying to disguise their location." He rubbed the back of his neck. "I'm so tired, I can't think clearly. At the speed they're coming, they'll overtake us long before we reach the business." He searched the darkness. "There's only one thing we can do. Get out of sight and pray they'll keep following Ethan's tracks."

While there was plenty of underbrush around, Leora wondered, if they managed to escape this time, how many more chances would they be given?

"Which way?"

"Over there. The brush appears the thickest." Fletcher looked along the path they'd been traveling. "Molly's too far ahead for me to get her attention without alerting those people."

They found a place and crouched low. Leora instinctively reached for his hand.

Fletcher looked into her eyes. "It's going to be *oke*." He brushed gentle fingers across her cheek. The tenderness in his eyes swept her away to a safer place where hope burned bright, and the future didn't seem so dark. She closed her eyes and searched for calm, for the strength to make it through this moment. More than anything, she wished they could disappear from this dangerous situation unfolding around them.

SEVEN

Fletcher held Leora and prayed he hadn't lied to her. If these people discovered their hiding place, things wouldn't be okay. Far from it.

Leora inched nearer as several people marched through the trees by their location. None of the men advancing spoke. They knew he and Leora were close, and they didn't want to alert them.

His heart sank. He'd gone through countless search and rescue missions in the mountains. Had listened to Ethan's stories about recon missions in Afghanistan. He'd taken them farther into the woods because he'd believed that would be what Ethan would do, when he should have walked out and found a way to reach Sheriff Collins. Instead, he'd allowed Molly to track Ethan, and he'd put their lives in jeopardy multiple times for what? They still didn't know what had happened to Ethan or where Tanner was.

The footsteps advanced. He and Leora might

be forced to stand and defend themselves should their hiding place be discovered.

Fletcher leaned in and whispered against Leora's ear, "We have to be ready."

She jerked toward him, her eyes wide and fearful.

Fletcher pulled out the weapon he'd wrestled from the guard earlier. "No matter what happens, stay behind me."

She swallowed before slowly nodding.

Fletcher tried to determine how many people were coming their way. At least three—probably a whole lot more. Far too many to take on by themselves, but if it came to it, he'd do it.

Through the darkness, he spotted one of the men far too close to their hiding spot.

A prayer slipped from silent lips. After what had happened between him and Catherine, he'd spent many an hour praying. Asking *Gott* for guidance.

The man moved forward still. *No. Oh, no.* His foot landed a few feet from where they crouched. It was too late to run. Fletcher slowly raised the weapon, ready to fire.

"Peters, come in. We have him!" Jade's voice came through a walkie-talkie. It held excitement. Fletcher still remembered her barking angry orders at her men earlier. This was different. Something had happened.

The man called Peters stopped. "Repeat, please. You have who?"

Fletcher's heart threatened to explode. Their fate had been so certain a second earlier.

"We have Tanner Mast."

Fletcher cut his eyes to Leora. Her devastation was clear.

"Copy that," Peters said with satisfaction. "What about Connors? He's still out there somewhere, presenting a huge threat."

"There's no sign of him yet. He's had extensive military training, and he knows these woods. Still, he can't hide forever. We'll get him soon enough. Tanner is hurt. I need you and your people here immediately. We're transporting him to the location."

"What about the two Amish people? We're close. I feel it. There's a good chance they've seen some of our faces, and they know enough to cause trouble."

"Don't worry about them." Jade's voice came through deadly clear. "They'll never walk out of these woods alive."

Fletcher struggled to keep himself from reacting. Tanner had been captured. If Ethan hadn't managed to call for help or escape, then it was up to him and Leora to stay alive long enough to save his friend and Tanner.

"Fine, we're on our way. Where are you?"

Jade gave him their location in longitude and latitude readings. Peters stepped away, and Fletcher could breathe again. "You heard her. Let's go."

The group of men headed away from their hiding place. A welcomed relief, but his concern for Leora's *bruder* had skyrocketed.

Fletcher waited until their movements had faded before he rose and reached for Leora's hand. "We need to catch up with Molly and get to the logging business."

Leora didn't answer. He couldn't imagine how she must be feeling knowing these terrible people had Tanner.

"Once we reach the building, we can call in the sheriff and his people. We'll find Ethan, and then we'll get your *bruder* back."

His assurances didn't ease the broken expression on her face. "They'll continue to look for Ethan as well as us. How will we ever manage to escape them?"

He stopped walking and faced her. "Because we're not giving up. This isn't how things are supposed to end, Leora. It's not how we're supposed to end," he stressed when her doubts were clear. He took her hand in his. "We have to keep fighting for Tanner and Ethan. For us."

She searched his face before agreeing. "You're right. We keep fighting."

He smiled at the strength he saw in her. Despite her physical frailties, she wouldn't give up.

"Where do you think Molly has gone?" Leora asked as they picked up the trail they'd been walking.

"I believe she's still on Ethan's scent and somewhere up ahead. If she keeps on this path, she'll hit the logging business soon."

Though he didn't dare use the flashlight, Fletcher periodically stopped to lean down and search the ground until he picked up Molly's tracks.

"I'm so scared for my *bruder*. Where do you think they would take him?"

Fletcher had thought about this for a while. This national forest was vast, with over two million acres to hide. Yet there were pockets of private land scattered around. "It could be any number of places. They may have even transported him out of the wilderness. Wherever it is, I believe it's someplace which isn't well traveled."

Leora looked even more discouraged. "In other words, he could be anywhere. How will we ever find him?"

"First step is to get the sheriff involved. Then we call in the search and rescue team. One step at a time." But, like her, he couldn't help but sense the situation seemed impossible.

Fletcher did his best to think about something else. The last time he'd been through here had been a few years back. Coming from a logging background himself, Fletcher had been impressed with the way such a large business ran so smoothly. He'd taken a tour of the place to see if there were some way he and his family could improve their own logging company.

The underbrush rustled off to their right. Fletcher drew the weapon and pushed Leora behind him. When Molly emerged, he bent over in relief.

Molly stopped in front of him. He patted the dog's head.

"She came back for us." Leora sounded surprised.

"In her military career, she was trained never to leave a soldier behind." He glanced her way. "I sure hope with the rain she hasn't lost Ethan's trail." He pulled out the scrap of fabric and held it to the dog's nose.

Once Molly had the scent identified, it didn't take her long to get back on track. He and Leora rushed to keep up with her while Fletcher wondered what they would find when they finally located Ethan. An injured friend? Or something far worse?

We have Tanner Mast.

Her stomach had instantly become a ball

of nerves from the moment she'd heard those dreadful words.

"They need him alive for now," Fletcher said as if reading her troubled thoughts.

"I know." At least her head believed they couldn't kill Tanner until they had whatever it was they claimed he'd taken. But how long before they were able to break him?

Leora kept replaying every single conversation she'd had with her *bruder,* hoping to understand what she might be missing. There had to be something.

Looking back in light of everything that had happened, Leora wondered why she hadn't thought to question Tanner further about his lost phones. He'd told her his phone was a lifeline to his employer and a necessary part of his job. Losing something so valuable wasn't like him. Her twin was usually much more responsible with his possessions.

She remembered the knife that had once belonged to their *daed.* If Tanner had managed to conceal the knife as Fletcher had his, he would at least have a way to protect himself. She held on to this hope while her mind kept racing over possible outcomes.

"I need something to take my mind off what might be happening to my *bruder.* Do you mind if we go over what we know so far?"

He smiled, and she realized despite everything they were going through, he had a nice smile. She wanted to see more of it—preferably under different circumstances. "Actually, I was thinking the same thing. Let's start in the beginning—at least the beginning as we know it. Which has to be…"

"With Tanner," she finished for him. Leora scrubbed her palm across her forehead.

"Exactly. Knowing everything you do now, when was the first time you noticed something might be troubling Tanner?"

"It's easy to see now. The lost phones. Tanner was never careless with his things. I can see misplacing one phone, but three? It doesn't add up. And my *bruder* would never abandon his truck willingly. I'm almost certain Tanner wasn't the one who sent the text to his employer saying he was quitting."

She glanced down at her simple blue dress caked with mud. "The first thing I want to do when we're safe is take a bath. I feel icky, and I must look horrible."

Fletcher chuckled. "You could never look horrible. You look like someone who has survived much."

She flinched at what he'd said. He had no way of knowing she was a survivor of much.

Fletcher tucked an escaping strand of hair

behind her ear without thinking. She inhaled a quick breath and bit down on her bottom lip while telling herself he was only being kind.

"We've both been through a lot. I had no idea when I heard those shots this morning—or I should say yesterday morning—I would end up meeting you in Ethan's panic room." He shook his head. "Or we'd end up being kidnapped and running for our lives."

Leora had known when she'd made the trip that something was dreadfully wrong. She'd hoped to find both Ethan and Tanner safe in Montana. Instead, she had no idea what was happening. "If only I'd asked more questions. I might have been able to help Tanner—at least prevent what's happened." Her mind recalled the night Tanner had stayed over at her place. He'd checked the doors multiple times to make sure they were locked. When he wasn't checking them, he was watching out the window, as if expecting someone to show up. And he'd lied about visiting their great-aunt and -uncle. Where had he gone?

"I don't believe Tanner would ever do anything illegal. He may have gotten into some minor trouble when he was younger, but he would never break the law. Even though he left our faith, Tanner still loves *Gott*, and he loves his country."

"Considering these people have kidnapped

us, not only threatening our lives but obviously Tanner's and Ethan's, I'd say they're the ones who broke the law. Perhaps Tanner figured out what they were up to and was trying to prevent it somehow."

Leora hadn't considered Tanner might be trying to stop a crime from happening.

"You said you recognized the one man's voice from your house. What about Jade? Do you know her?"

Leora shook her head. "I don't know how she fits into everything."

Fletcher mentioned the footprints again that Jade had basically ignored.

Leora tried to understand why Jade hadn't pursued them until they'd been captured. "She definitely appeared to be the one calling the shots at Ethan's house and then again just now."

Fletcher frowned, his attention on Molly, who had her nose down. "Whatever these men believe Tanner has taken is valuable enough for them to go to such dangerous extremes. Right now, it's Tanner's only advantage. Once they know where your *bruder* hid whatever they're looking for, they won't have any reason to keep him or any of us alive."

Leora shivered at the image while fear and tension made her muscles ache. "How much farther until we reach the logging business?"

Molly veered off the path they were on, forcing Leora and Fletcher to trudge through heavy undergrowth to keep her in sight.

Once the German shepherd was back on track, Fletcher returned his attention to Leora. "We have to be within a few miles. How are you feeling?"

She hated telling people about the cancer and seeing the pity in their looks. Hated thinking about what lay ahead should this last round of chemo not work out. "I'm simply tired. This has been a lot." Her hand swept their surroundings.

He took her at her word and didn't ask questions. "Let's take a short break."

Though they were running out of time, she wasn't sure how much farther she could go on traipsing blindly through the woods. She nodded relieved. "Yes, but only for a second or two."

Fletcher glanced around for some place to sit. "It appears a soggy log is the best I can offer."

She smiled at the way he tried to lighten the moment and sat on the log while ignoring the uncomfortable moisture soaking into her clothes and boring through her skin. The situation felt hopeless. It was hard not to give up and cry.

Take your mind off what's troubling you, Leora. Her *daed*'s words came to mind. At times she could almost picture his smiling face still. More than anything, she wished she had him to talk to about what had happened to Tanner.

Losing her parents had been hard enough, but then she'd been forced to leave the only home she'd ever known. Before Leora had had time to settle into life in Colorado, Tanner left the Amish faith. Not having her twin close had made the loss of her parents that much harder.

Each night for months following their deaths, Leora would cry herself to sleep. And the guilt she'd felt over not being able to apologize for her reckless behavior had become crippling at times. She'd needed her *bruder*, only Tanner was gone. Weeks went by before she'd even heard from him, and then it was a brief letter telling her he'd joined the marines and would be shipped to a war zone soon. Leora had been so frightened she'd lose him, too.

"We should keep going. Molly isn't letting up."

As much as she'd needed this break, Tanner's life was more important, as was Ethan's. No matter how tired she might be, she'd soldier through for them.

She rose and unstuck her skirt before falling into step beside Fletcher while she remembered how Tanner had called her during almost every single haulage trip he'd made. He'd tell her about all the different pieces of art he'd transported. Tanner had thought it funny how expensive several pieces he'd carried had been appraised for.

"Some are simply squiggly lines, Leora." He'd laughed as he'd described the different pieces. She'd loved hearing those stories. But then, everything started to change. Little changes at first, until the final visit.

Would she get her *bruder* back alive? Leora swallowed several times. She couldn't let herself think such things. Tanner was a strong man, and he'd trained under Ethan. She had to trust Tanner to be able to keep himself alive until they could reach him, because she couldn't lose him. She'd lost so much already. Her parents and grandparents. She couldn't lose Tanner. Because if she did, Leora wasn't so sure she would make it through such a loss.

After the cancer had returned for the second time, Leora had accepted that she would never fall in love or have a family of her own. How could she ask someone to go through dealing with the cancer when there was the chance she might die?

Leora realized Fletcher was watching her—probably seeing more than she wanted. She cleared her throat. "How long have you and your family lived in these parts?" she asked to chase away the ghosts from her thoughts. Leora tried to recall what Ethan had told her about his partners. She knew they were Amish and he'd become *gut* friends with them through some difficult situations.

"For a very long time," he said with amusement in his tone. "My *grossdaddi* was the one who started our family's logging business when he was quite young. He bought several hundred acres of land near the community. The business did well. *Grossdaddi* loved making furniture, and so he turned the logging portion over to his *sohn* and went back to making furniture. Soon, he was making furniture for *Englischers* around the area, then later, the state and beyond. He brought in my *bruder* Aaron to help, along with me." He shrugged. "It's *gut* work."

She repeated his last name in her head and realized she'd heard of the Shetler furniture makers. "I've seen some of your family's pieces at a store in Pagosa Springs. They were lovely. Your family is very talented."

He inclined his head. "*Denki*. It's nice to hear our work is appreciated, but it also makes me laugh when I think of my *bruder* and myself creating those pieces. Aaron and I were always getting into trouble growing up—exploring when we should have been working." He shook his head. "I'm sure our parents wondered if we'd ever figure it out."

She liked the way his face lit up when he spoke about his family and the West Kootenai community. They were important to him. Family was what bound the Amish together. At one time, she'd felt the same way. Until her parents had died.

Now, at times, it felt as if death was the one thing to hold her and Tanner together.

"It must be nice to have such a large family to lean on."

He looked at her curiously. "It is. Aaron is passing along the skills we learned from our *grossdaddi* to his *sohn*. The family work will continue. We don't see it as a talent but a skill."

He was a humble man.

"And now you and your brother Mason are working as hunting guides and doing search and rescue missions. Quite a leap from a furniture maker."

Fletcher smiled and kept his eye on Molly's progress as they continued through the thick brush. "I guess it is. Mason and I both enjoy what we do as guides. We're not just teaching those who we take out how to hunt properly, but how to use every part of the animal who sacrificed its life. We don't allow hunters who are strictly hoping for trophy kills." The enthusiasm in his voice was easy to hear.

"It must be nice to follow your dreams. I'd be too afraid I'd fail." She hadn't always been so cautious. At one time, she couldn't wait to explore the world. Until she'd lost her family.

"I suppose. I still help my *bruder* with the furniture business, and I look after our *mamm*. As much as I enjoy being a guide, it's the search and rescues we perform, which are the most meaningful. It makes me feel as if I'm doing something important."

She could understand. Growing up, her *daed* had talked about how important it was to do something for others. He'd always been there to help his neighbors in their small Ruby Valley community, and it didn't matter if they were Amish or not.

"Do you enjoy working at the fabric shop?" Fletcher asked curiously.

Leora let the past return to its resting place. Thinking about the life she'd lived with her parents in Ruby Valley made her wish she could return there again, if only for a little while.

"*Jah*, I do. My employer, Martha Cooper, is a kind woman. She doesn't have any family, so she's pretty much adopted me."

Leora's future was settled. She had her work. Her family and a few friends. Yet she'd once dreamed of marrying. Having a houseful of *kinner*…until she'd lost the man she'd loved. Then the blows had kept coming with the cancer diagnosis. At first, she'd been floored. When her doctor had told her they'd caught it in time, she'd believed everything would work out. Through every single round of chemo, she'd told herself it would all work out. And it had for a little while. Until her cancer returned.

"Leora?"

She realized she'd missed whatever Fletcher had been saying. "I'm sorry, I was thinking of something."

He searched her face, probably seeing far too much. "Martha sounds like a nice woman."

Leora smiled. "She is. She has taught me so much." One day she would take over the shop for Martha.

If you live long enough.

The truth always had a way of slapping her in the face.

"That's sad she doesn't have anyone. We aren't meant to be alone."

There was something in his tone. She turned toward him.

"Family is important to you, isn't it? Do you want a family one day?" Leora immediately regretted the question. It was too personal and not her place to ask. "I'm sorry. I shouldn't have…"

His jaw tightened. "It's *oke*." Yet he stared

straight ahead, his profile rigid. She wondered what secrets he kept to himself.

"At one time, I thought I would have a *fraa* and a family. Only it wasn't meant to be, so I remain alone. *Gott*'s path isn't ours to change."

"You really believe that?" For reasons she couldn't explain, it made her sad to think of him alone.

Up ahead, Molly had stopped short and appeared to key in on something.

She and Fletcher hurried to the dog.

"What is it, girl?" He leaned down to inspect what the shepherd had found. "Footprints. Only a single set. This is a *gut* sign Ethan is on the move." He looked up at Leora. "Ethan's injuries can't be so severe if he's able to keep going." He patted the dog's head and straightened. "Ethan is strong. He'll be *oke*."

She wondered which of them he was trying to convince the most.

Molly didn't waste time getting back on her track, and they quickly followed.

"Ethan told me some stories about things he and his team had gone through while in service. Some of the missions were rough." He brought in a breath. "I can't even imagine going through half of those things."

Tanner didn't usually like to speak about being in the war, but on occasion, he'd talk about the Afghan people who had been affected. The innocent ones were those who haunted him the most.

Something shifted in the woods to the left of them. Leora grabbed his arm. "There's someone over there," she whispered.

Fletcher pulled her behind a tree as the sound grew louder and much more defined. There had to be half a dozen people tromping through the brush.

Several of the men came close enough to where Leora believed they had to be standing right beside the tree she and Fletcher hid behind.

Tension raced through her body. Why weren't the men moving? Once more, they weren't using flashlights, which she hoped prevented them from seeing her and Fletcher's footprints.

After what felt like forever, the group eventually continued on. Even after the quiet returned to the countryside, neither she nor Fletcher moved. Leora didn't trust this not to be a trick. Those men might be trying to lure them out of hiding.

"Stay here. I'll see if it's safe to continue," Fletcher said against her ear before untangling arms.

Before he'd taken a single step, another sound behind them had them both whirling toward it, fearing the worst. When Molly appeared nearby, Leora almost dropped to the ground from relief.

"She heard the men and came to protect us. Good girl." Fletcher praised the dog before ordering her to stay with Leora.

"Please, be careful."

Fletcher looked into her eyes, and her heart beat a crazy rhythm that had nothing to do with fear. "I will," he whispered in an unsteady tone. With a final searching look, Fletcher stepped away.

She squeezed her eyes shut. Leora didn't understand what was happening to her. She and Fletcher had only met. Yet despite the danger pressing in on all sides, she felt something for Fletcher she hadn't believed possible.

With him gone, Leora knelt beside the dog and hugged her close while a prickle of unease slipped through her limbs. Molly growled low, reinforcing Leora's troubled feeling. There was something nearby. Leora searched the soggy darkness around her and tried to see what waited there.

"What is it, girl?"

A shape shifted within the trees. She rose unsteadily and jumped back when someone stepped from the darkness and charged for her.

Molly bound for the intruder, taking him by surprise.

"Molly, no." Leora feared the man would kill the dog.

She wanted to call for Fletcher. But would that bring more armed men to her location?

Leora reached the man, who was trying to get the dog off him, and shoved him hard. He stumbled backward and tried to keep his footing. A heartbeat later, Molly charged him once more. The man pulled something from his pocket and leveled it at Molly.

A gun.

He fired at the dog, missing her by a breath.

Molly latched onto his leg. He shrieked in pain as Leora grabbed for the weapon. Despite the dog's attack, he managed to hold on to the gun.

As she continued to try to free the weapon from his clutches, the man kicked at Molly hard. The dog let go of his leg. He grabbed hold of Leora and dragged her up against him while shoving the weapon next to her head. "Call the dog off or I'll shoot."

Desperate, Leora smashed the heel of her shoe against his foot. The man raged out expletives and released her.

"Run, Molly." Leora ducked low and followed the dog. The man fired off a shot. It flew past Leora's shoulder, confirming he didn't care if she lived or died.

Leora kept running while praying for *Gott*'s protection. Molly stopped suddenly and then raced past her, toward the man again.

"No, Molly." She reached a tree and ducked behind it. The man hadn't followed. He was wrestling with someone else. Fletcher. Molly dove into the middle of the two men. The stranger reacted by trying to shove the dog away, momentarily giving Fletcher the upper hand.

"Fletcher, he has a gun," Leora yelled and ran to assist.

Fletcher swung something in his hand. The gun he'd taken before. It struck the man on the side of the head and he dropped to his knees. Another blow had him falling to the ground unconscious.

Fletcher grabbed the man's weapon. He searched his pockets and found, like with the previous man, there was no cell phone. Just a walkie-talkie. It would be useless in reaching anyone from the outside world, and it might lead their pursuers to their location.

"Let's get out of here." Fletcher handed Leora the second weapon he just took. "The others will have heard the noise and will come to investigate."

They ran back in the direction Leora had come while Molly shot past them.

The cold burned her lungs, but she did her best to keep up while looking behind them, expecting the bad guys to materialize behind them shooting.

It wasn't long before the rush of multiple footsteps heading their way drowned out her labored breathing. Her feet stumbled beneath her, and she fought to catch herself before she fell.

Fletcher clasped her hand. "I've got you. I've got you."

EIGHT

The intense darkness immediately swallowed up the dog from sight. Fletcher kept on the path while praying Molly hadn't veered off in a different direction.

He held firmly onto Leora's hand as they continued to run through the pitch-black woods. They couldn't stop even though his ankle throbbed painfully. No matter what, they had to stay one step ahead of those men.

His mind raced over the details he knew. Above all else, he didn't understand why Ethan hadn't gone out of the woods and called for help. Ethan knew this country like the back of his hand. He'd know going deeper into the woods wasn't the fastest way to achieve the goal.

"I think it's safe to slow down."

Leora didn't respond, and he looked over at her. She appeared to be struggling to breathe normally. Fletcher was really worried about her.

He put his arm around her shoulders to steady her. "I wish we could afford to stop."

She shook her head. "I'll be *oke*. I just need to catch my breath."

By now, they'd have found their friend. This was only a moment of reprieve. They'd keep coming.

Where was the logging company? They should have reached it by now.

Fragments of what Fletcher knew for certain and what he and Leora had gone through repeated in his head. The exhaustion went far beyond physical. His brain couldn't process things properly, and he desperately needed to make sense of what was happening. One thing in particular troubled him. How had Ethan and Tanner gotten separated in the first place? He shared his concerns with Leora.

Leora dragged in several deep breaths before responding. "If they were both together at Sam's and managed to escape, then something had to happen after they left the house." Her voice was little more than a whisper. She needed to conserve her strength.

Fletcher returned to his troubled thoughts. There were far greater things to be worried about. Jade's people would actively be searching for whatever they believed Tanner had taken. They'd have people in Colorado, as well. It was only a matter of time before they found it on their own, and when they did, Tanner's life would be worthless. And so would theirs and Ethan's.

"Look, the woods are thinning." Leora nodded up ahead.

When he spotted the clearing up ahead, his relief was great. "We're close to the logging company. Look, there's the road."

At least walking it would be easier than tromping through underbrush. Unfortunately, it would make them more visible.

"Where's Molly?" Leora looked around for the dog.

"She's probably reached the business by now. If she finds Ethan, she'll come back to alert us." The dog constantly impressed Fletcher by her skills. He thought about the pups in training. They had plenty of food to last them for a few days, and their water would last as long, but they'd grow restless without their usual training routine.

The woods had been cleared away. Lights illuminated the business grounds. An uneasy feeling had Fletcher glancing nervously around. It felt as if they had a spotlight on them compared to the darkness they'd come through.

Fletcher remembered the person who had given them the tour had told them they'd occasionally had problems with pieces of equipment disappearing. He understood the reason for the lights but still… A shiver worked through his frame. If those men were close, they'd spot them easy enough.

Up ahead, the milling facility appeared. Beyond it, the company's warehouse, where the cut lumber was stored, also housed the offices.

"There's Molly." He noticed the dog rounding the side of the warehouse.

Leora shot him a look. "Maybe she's found Ethan."

Please let it be. "I sure hope you're right." They followed the dog's trail. Once they reached the spot where Molly had disappeared from sight, Fletcher froze. A small side door stood open. Fletcher retrieved his weapon and waited for Leora to do the same. "Stay behind me." After she was in place, he slowly eased through the opening.

A cavernous space spread out before them filled with stacks and stacks of lumber. The scent of cut boards was familiar and one Fletcher loved.

There weren't any windows in this part of the warehouse. Fletcher clicked on the flashlight and shone it around. Molly stood beside something on the floor. Fletcher's heart leaped into his throat. *No, please no.* He rushed over and knelt. A bloody piece of flannel, as if someone had discarded a bandage.

Leora stared down at the blood-stained cloth and covered her mouth.

Fletcher had no doubt it belonged to his friend. "Let's search the building. If he's hurt badly, he could have hidden out of sight to wait for the business to open."

With Leora close, he and Molly finished searching the warehouse and found no other sign of Ethan. In Fletcher's mind, it was a good sign Ethan's injury hadn't been gravely serious.

"The offices are past those double doors." Fletcher headed into what he remembered as the reception area. The phone was displayed on the counter. *Oh, thank You,* Gott.

He couldn't reach it fast enough. He picked up the receiver, and it was like a punch to the gut. "There's no dial tone." Leora's frustration mirrored his. Fletcher couldn't accept they'd come so far only to have these results. He tried the phone again with the same result.

"The weather shouldn't affect the service," Leora said thoughtfully.

She was right. "Let's check the rest of the offices. Maybe it's only this phone." Yet, after a thorough search of the remaining offices, the results were the same.

"I don't understand." Fletcher's exhausted

mind tried to think of a solution. "Wait, maybe it's in the connection outside." He and Leora stepped out into the rain and searched until they found the phone box. The door stood open. Wires hung all around. Someone had deliberately cut the lines.

There would be no calling for help here.

Leora looked to him for answers he couldn't give.

He couldn't get the bloody cloth bandage out of his mind. "At one point, Ethan was here, and so were those men."

"What if they found him?"

Fletcher couldn't accept this as an answer. His gut told him Ethan was still out there somewhere, but he was clearly injured.

Before he could put the dog on Ethan's scent again, a noise near the milling facility turned his blood cold.

Someone was coming.

The dog started toward the sound, ready to defend them, but Fletcher grabbed Molly's collar. "Stay," he whispered. Molly reluctantly obeyed.

Fletcher eased along the wall until he was able to peek around the side. At least four men stood guard outside the milling plant. There would be others inside. His and Leora's window of escape was quickly closing.

He returned to Leora. "They'll reach this building soon enough. If we don't leave now, we'll be captured. This way." He started for the rear, which backed into the encroaching woods.

Once he reached the back of the building, Fletcher edged far enough away to see. Nothing appeared in his line of sight.

"Let me go first." He saw the concern in Leora's eyes and framed her face with his hands. "Once I reach the woods, you and Molly come after me."

She slowly nodded, and he skimmed her pretty face, memorizing every detail, before he let her go.

With another quick look at the milling facility, Fletcher stepped from his cover and closed the space between the office and the woods in two strides.

A relieved sigh slipped from his lips. Fletcher turned back to Leora and waved her forward.

He could see how nervous she was as she stepped from the building's cover and ran toward him, Molly keeping stride.

"Stop right there!" Sam yelled when he spotted Leora. Her terrified eyes latched onto Fletcher's, and she became frozen in place.

He couldn't let her die. Fletcher stepped from the woods and grabbed Leora's hand, pulling her along with him while Molly bounded in front of them.

With her hand tucked in his, Fletcher ran as fast as they both could physically. Multiple footsteps entered the woods behind them.

They were in real trouble. Fletcher tried to clear his weary mind enough to gain his bearings. If memory served him correctly, the mountains were close. As *kinner,* he and his *bruders* had played in the caves carved into the mountains. If they could reach the caves…

Fletcher told Leora his plan. "Our only option is to reach them before they catch up with us."

Leora's face reflected how much she was struggling. He placed his arm around her waist and helped her along while once more wondering what was wrong with her.

"Up ahead," a different man yelled. Less than a heartbeat later, the woods exploded with the sound of gunfire. Fletcher pulled Leora behind a tree. Both had weapons, but they couldn't hold back an army for long.

"We can't stay here. Keep in front of me." He pointed directly ahead. "Don't run in a straight line. Go, Leora."

She started running. Fletcher jumped out behind her and kept himself between Leora and the gunshots coming their way.

His breath pumped from his body. Fletcher

couldn't bring himself to look behind them. If they were going to die here in these woods, he didn't want to see the bullet coming.

Soon, the shooting stopped. He forced himself to catch up with Leora.

"We have to change directions." He somehow got the words out. "We're heading away from the caves ."

As they continued to run blindly through the trees, the ground slowly began to rise under their feet.

Fletcher finally forced himself to look over his shoulder. The lights were still heading in the direction he and Leora had been going. Their pursuers hadn't realized they'd veered to the right. For now, they appeared to have lost the men. Still, it was best to get out of sight as fast as possible.

Leora's breathing had grown worse. As much as he didn't want to stop, he wasn't sure how much farther she could go without a break.

"You need to take a moment to catch your breath. Over there." They reached a group of lodgepole pines growing close together and took cover.

Leora leaned over and sucked in breaths. Her color scared him.

"What's going on, Leora?"

She straightened and slowly was able to get

her breathing somewhat normal. "Nothing is going on. I told you, it was the trip to Montana coupled with what we've gone through. I'm fine now. Let's keep going."

He didn't believe her, but he kept his doubts to himself and started walking. He'd wait for her to trust him with the truth.

"That was so close." Leora said as they kept walking.

"*Jah*, it was." Fletcher stopped suddenly when he recalled the old gas station. He couldn't believe he hadn't thought of it before.

"What is it?"

He explained about the station. "It's located down the road from the logging company. They have a phone, or at least they used to."

Leora grabbed his arm and pointed. More lights were coming through the woods behind them.

"They must have radioed for backup." Fletcher's heart sank. Time was critical. If they couldn't reach the caves before those men caught up with them, everything they'd gone through would be pointless.

The trees thinned at the higher altitude. Soon, the sheer face of the mountain rose up before them like a wall. Finding one of the old caves, even though it was growing light out, it still wouldn't be easy. It had been years since he'd been inside them.

"Which way?" Leora asked while keeping a careful eye on the advancing lights.

Fletcher hesitated. He couldn't afford to be wrong. "Over there." He was almost positive this was the direction of the caves…but the margin for error was razor thin.

"I see something." Leora bobbed her head at a darker area on the mountainside. She and Fletcher went over to investigate.

"It doesn't look as if the entrance has caved in, or anyone's been by here recently. A *gut* thing."

Leora stared at the dark opening and didn't feel the same way. "Is it safe?"

"I sure hope so."

Not exactly the assurance she'd hoped for.

"Why don't you stay out here while I check inside? If you see anything, come get me." Fletcher hesitated, no doubt seeing all her fears.

She shivered at the thought of being alone but tried not to show it. "Go, I'll be fine."

"Keep Molly with you for protection." He turned and ducked down low before disappearing through the entrance.

Leora prayed they would find the shelter they

needed to rest because she wasn't sure how much longer she could keep going.

She watched the lights below. So far, they didn't appear to be following her and Fletcher's footprints.

Fletcher had returned without her realizing it and she jumped. Her hand flew to her chest where her heart raced.

"Sorry," he told her. "It appears safe enough. We can get out of the elements for a bit." He nodded toward the lights. "Looks like they aren't on our trail yet."

Molly went through the entrance first. Fletcher clasped her hand. "I can't afford to use the flashlight until we're inside. Watch your step."

She ducked low, like Fletcher. The ground beneath their feet was barely visible. Pieces of the wall had sloughed away and littered the ground they walked.

The temperature changed dramatically as they pushed deeper inside the mountain.

"We should be able to use the flashlight now." Fletcher clicked it on. The reality of what surrounded them was far worse than Leora had imagined.

"I know it doesn't look good, but we're out of the elements and it's dry. And we're safe."

She slowly collected herself. "You're right."

Yet the cobwebs and dust surrounding her, along with the dank smell, made it hard to feel safe.

"If I'm remembering correctly, there's a large open area further down this passage." Fletcher continued along the narrow corridor until they reached a large circular space.

"Sit and rest," Fletcher told her gently. "I'm going to see if there's another way out."

She grabbed his arm, her eyes wide and fearful. After everything they'd been through, the thought of being alone, even for a second, was terrifying.

"I won't be long, I promise." She was tired and giving in to her fears. Leora slowly let him go and sank to the ground while fighting back tears.

Fletcher took off his coat once more and slipped it over her shoulders. "I will be warm enough in here," he assured her when she would have protested.

With him gone, she struggled to keep it together. She'd been on an emotional journey for weeks. Had prayed everything would be resolved once she reached Ethan's house, but nothing could be further from the truth.

Leora brushed the tears away angrily. *Stop it.* She'd gotten through bouts with cancer and hadn't cried a single tear. She wouldn't now. Tanner and Ethan needed her to be strong.

She pulled her knees up against her chin and prayed for courage she didn't feel right now.

Only a few minutes passed before Fletcher and the dog returned. The expression on Fletcher's face wasn't good.

"There's no other way out," she said when he sank down beside her.

"Not one we can use anyway. It's collapsed over time. It would take far too long to get it unblocked."

She couldn't find a response.

"How are you feeling?" He turned his head toward her. Once more, Leora was struck by how handsome Fletcher was, and not simply physically. He had a kind heart. She'd seen it displayed many times during their time together.

She slowly smiled. "I'm making it. How about you? You have to be exhausted, and your poor ankle…"

The tenderness in his eyes warmed her inside. "I've been better, but then I think we both can say as much." He chuckled while his attention went to her hair.

Leora involuntarily reached up to pat it down. "I must look a mess."

He shook his head, the same gentle smile on his face. "You are a beautiful and strong woman."

Her breath stuck in her throat. Their eyes held. Something passed between them.

Yet, even after surviving two serious health challenges, she believed her life had a time stamp. She couldn't put anyone through watching her die.

Fletcher cleared his throat, breaking the emotional silence. "Some of your color has returned. You look much better."

She flinched.

"Sorry, I didn't mean it to come out like that." Fletcher had seen her reaction. "You are an attractive woman even when you're tired."

He thought she was being vain. Leora waved her hand in front of her and searched for something to say to change the subject. "How did you and Ethan first meet?"

Fletcher's expression relaxed as if he knew she wanted to shift things off herself. "We actually met through my *bruder* Aaron after Ethan bought some of our furniture for his place here. He and I discovered we had a lot in common, and we became *gut* friends. When Mason came back to West Kootenai, we decided to move forward with our childhood dream of opening our own guide business." He shrugged when Leora looked at him curiously.

He watched Molly circle around several times before claiming her spot nearby. "We brought

Ethan in, and he's been a wonderful addition to our team. Ethan had been doing search and rescue missions for a while and invited us to help. When Ethan mentioned wanting to train rescue dogs…well, I was all-in."

"Working with the dogs must be fulfilling."

He looked her way. "It is. Though it has been a bit time consuming with the guide business and doing our search and rescue missions. I'm rarely home. Although I enjoy making furniture and still help out my *bruder* from time to time, Aaron and his *sohn* are the future for the furniture-making business—not me." He shook his head. "With Mason's mother-in-law suffering from an illness, he spends more time with his growing family. It is sad seeing someone you care about slowly fade away. I don't know how Mason does it. I'm not so sure I could watch someone I love die."

Leora couldn't take her eyes off him. *I'm not so sure I could watch someone I love die.* She couldn't blame him. Not too many people could.

"What's wrong with her?" Her voice came out strained.

"She has Huntington's."

Though Leora knew so very little about the disease, it was Fletcher's words that stuck in her head.

Fletcher's attention dropped to the dog once

more. "At one time, I imagined my life would look like Mason's. A *fraa* and a family. Until…"

Leora was mesmerized by the pain on his face. "What happened between you two?" she asked softly.

His sharp gaze found her again. "Catherine chose someone else. She wanted to leave the community. I didn't. She found someone who would take her away." Fletcher rose and dusted off his clothes. "I should look around outside. I can find my way out. You keep the flashlight." With Molly at his heels, he headed off through the makeshift opening. She hadn't missed the catch in his voice she recognized so well.

So many things shaped the way a person's life turned out. Whom they trusted—whom they loved. It only took one dreadful blow to change the course of a life. Hers had started long before her cancer appeared. Once more, her restless behavior during *Rumspringa* haunted her. *Mamm* and *Daed* had been so disappointed in Leora. At the time, she hadn't cared…until she'd lost them. Everything changed then. She still carried the guilt with her every day. What she wouldn't give to be able to say she was sorry to her parents for all that she'd put them through.

Fletcher returned with the dog, and she struggled to let go of the heartbreaking past.

"They appear to have followed the rest of the

men. We should leave while we have the advantage. I'm sorry—I wish we had more time, but Ethan's and Tanner's lives are in danger."

Leora slowly rose. "It's *oke*. There'll be time to rest when we find them."

Fletcher smiled. "It's going to be a bit of a hike to the gas station, but it's the most logical choice where Ethan would head to use the phone. I'm guessing the phones had already been disabled when he arrived at the logging business."

Leora bent and grabbed the flashlight. "That makes sense." She handed it to Fletcher.

"I'd better turn it off. How's your wrist doing?"

She realized she hadn't thought about her sprained wrist in a bit. "Much better." She tested it. "How's your ankle and your shoulder and—"

He laughed. "All injuries are still there but cooperating for the moment."

"*Gut* to know." She liked the way his laugh lit up his face and took away some of the worry. Leora wondered what it would be like had they met under different circumstances.

"Here, take my hand. It's a bit difficult through here." She slipped her hand in his. The calluses were a reminder of the hard work this man did.

Fletcher clicked off the flashlight before they

reached the entrance. An intense darkness so great it seemed physical pressed in. He waited a second for their eyes to adjust. "Ready?"

She nodded and then realized he couldn't see her reaction. "*Jah*, I'm ready."

Fletcher kept her close as they felt their way through the opening and outside. Molly, accustomed to taking the lead, started down the mountainside.

The cold appeared to have intensified though the rain had stopped.

Leora searched the darkness below them. Not a single light. She listened and heard nothing but the noises of the woods. "Where are they?" she whispered.

Fletcher stopped to look at her. "I don't know, but I sure hope they kept going."

Molly sniffed at the air.

But why would those men keep moving when it was important for them to find her and Fletcher before they reached someone who could help? It didn't make sense. Unless something had happened.

Her thoughts went to her *bruder*. Had they gotten what they needed from Tanner? Her heart seized. She didn't want to think about Tanner's fate once that happened.

NINE

The dirt road running parallel to the logging business appeared in front of them. Fletcher stopped near the edge and looked both ways. So far, no sign of their chasers. The gas station was located farther up the road. It had been serving loggers for several decades. Fletcher remembered the older couple who ran the place, but it had been a few years since he'd visited the station.

"This way." He pointed right and they started walking.

Molly appeared to have picked up a scent. *Let it be Ethan's.*

"At some point, Ethan must have been down this way since Molly appears to be back on his trail." He watched the dog steadfastly track her owner.

"Maybe we'll find him at the station."

Fletcher hoped her words proved right, but he had a bad feeling whatever was actually happening here had a long way to go before being over.

Though it felt as if they'd been tromping through the woods forever, Fletcher tried to gauge the time. Probably several hours to go still before dawn.

As they continued down the road, placing one foot in front of the other proved all he was able to concentrate on. Would he be risking their lives by staying on the road? He was too tired to know anymore.

Shortly, the trees near the station, which had been cleared away from the road, appeared in front of them. "This is it." There was a light near the gas and diesel pumps and a single bulb over the entrance to the store.

Fletcher stopped at the edge of the trees, suddenly nervous. What if those men had somehow followed Ethan here? He didn't know how many people were out there altogether. He blew out a sigh. "Let's circle around behind the store to check it out."

Staying inside the trees, they eased through them until they reached the rear. Nothing stirred around the exterior.

Molly kept on her scent and moved past the building.

Fletcher faced Leora. "So far, so good." They stepped from the trees and reached the back entrance. Fletcher tried the door. Locked.

"Maybe Ethan found a different way inside?

He'd want to keep the doors locked to make it appear as normal as possible should those men pass this way."

It made sense…still. "Regardless of whether Ethan is inside or not, we've got to get to the phone."

After trying the front entrance and several windows with the same results, Fletcher realized he'd have to find a way to break the lock on the back door.

He flipped the flashlight over and slammed the butt against the lock. It took three tries before it snapped open. Fletcher removed the broken lock and opened the door.

With Leora close, he stepped into what appeared to be a storage room. Fletcher clicked on the light and searched around. No sign of Ethan.

Molly didn't stop at the rear entrance. Had Ethan kept going? It didn't make sense that he would.

Think. The phone had to be their top priority right now. He walked past the storage room lined with freezers and into the main store.

After a search around the aisles, it became clear Ethan had never been inside the store.

Fletcher's shoulders sagged. "He's not here and probably never has been." In the past, he remembered the phone had been behind the counter. He hurried over there and searched around.

There was no sign of a phone. "It's gone. Where could it be? The station is obviously still operational."

Leora searched for the phone, as well. "Maybe they got rid of it and only use their cell phone. Martha told me lots of businesses are going this way."

He tried not to fall apart. They'd come all this way—wasted time they didn't have—for nothing.

Fletcher noticed a pen and paper behind the counter and had an idea. He grabbed the pen and scribbled a desperate note to the owners explaining what had happened.

My name is Fletcher Shetler and I need you to call Sheriff Collins as soon as you read this note.

Fletcher wrote down everything he recalled and left the paper on the counter close to the cash register where it wouldn't be missed.

"We should grab some water and something to eat before we leave. I'll make sure to swing by the station and pay the owners once this is all over."

If they survived their ordeal.

Leora went over to the cooler and took out a

couple of bottled waters. "What about Molly? She has to be thirsty."

"Get an extra one for her." He grabbed a few bags of chips and handed one to her. "I'll check outside for the dog. She may still be following Ethan's trail."

Fletcher started through the freezer area when something alarming caught his attention. Flashlights. Moving through the woods behind the station.

Outside, he searched, found the destroyed lock and shoved it into his pocket before returning inside. Fletcher slid the dead bolt into place. It would offer only a small amount of resistance to someone determined to get in, but it was all they had.

He ran back through to Leora. "Get down." He ushered her behind the counter where they ducked low.

"Fletcher?" Leora's frightened gaze found him.

"They're coming. I did my best to hide that we're here. I hope it works."

Fletcher held her close, huddled together as multiple flashlights bounced all around the building. One man stepped up to the front and shone his light inside. Fletcher tucked Leora against the counter and prayed they wouldn't be spotted.

"There's no sign of them. Let's keep moving. He wants to wrap this up quickly and get out of here to keep the shipments on schedule."

To keep the shipments on schedule. The words replayed through Fletcher's mind. Did this all have something to do with the transportation business Tanner had worked for?

Within minutes, the men stepped away, and Fletcher rose. He walked over to the windows and looked out. "They're gone. We need to find Molly and keep going."

Fletcher glanced at the note and prayed the owners would find it in time to save them.

Stepping outside, Fletcher remembered Molly had been heading away from the station when he'd lost sight of her. They headed for her last location as Fletcher reached for Leora's hand, because he was worried about her, and he liked feeling her hand in his.

He'd gone through some harrowing situations with his *bruders* in the past, as well as during their search and rescue missions, but this was different. It was him and Leora against so many, and he didn't want to make a wrong decision that might cost them dearly.

Shots rang out in the direction they were heading. Molly yelped.

"I see Connors. He's up ahead," one of the men called to his partners.

They'd spotted Ethan.

"Oh, no," Leora whispered. "We have to go after them."

As they ran toward the sound of more shooting, movement nearby had them both whirling. Fletcher pushed Leora behind his frame for protection.

Molly emerged. Fletcher recalled the dog's yelp and rushed to investigate. "I don't see any new injuries. Maybe one of the men kicked her."

Molly quickly shook off Fletcher's hold and raced back into the bushes.

Fletcher glanced at Leora before following.

The shooting appeared to veer off into a different direction.

Molly stopped abruptly and sniffed the air before suddenly shifting direction.

"What's up this way?" Leora asked between breaths.

"Not much, if I remember correctly. Mostly woods."

If he remembered correctly there were a couple of *Englischer* properties some distance in this direction.

He and Leora practically had to run to keep up with the dog's fast pace.

Molly stopped and alerted to something on the ground. Fletcher reached the dog and saw a large amount of blood covering the grass.

"That's an awful lot," Leora said in a troubled voice.

Fletcher straightened and looked around. "He's been shot."

The shooting had stopped. With so much blood loss, Ethan could be passed out. Had the men found him already?

Up until now, he'd been certain his special ops friend could survive anything. Now, with this amount of blood…well, he wasn't nearly as sure.

As Molly continued her mission, he did his best not to think about what might have happened to Ethan.

Fletcher was pretty certain they were on private land now. He tried to recall who owned this particular piece. It had changed hands a few years back. He told Leora about the previous sale. "The owners aren't from around here, I believe."

Once more, Fletcher thought about the things he'd witnessed with his family. The remoteness of the area seemed to offer the perfect place for criminals to hide. This could be related to drugs. Human trafficking.

He remembered the comment about the shipment and voiced his concern.

She visibly shivered. "You think someone hijacked one of the shipments of art and plans to sell it on a black market?"

Fletcher wasn't sure what he thought at this point.

Gunshots ricocheted throughout the countryside. He and Leora dove for cover. His heart blasted an unsteady beat in his ears while he determined the direction. "It's coming from straight in front of us."

"Ethan." Leora looked up at him with troubled eyes. "He needs our help."

They ran toward the gunshots while Fletcher tried to recall the layout of the land. Another round of shots happened, followed by return fire. They stopped dead in their tracks.

"Wait—someone else is returning fire?" Leora's huge eyes met his.

"Ethan."

The shooting suddenly stopped and silence returned briefly, followed by a vehicle's engine firing up.

Molly had disappeared completely. Fletcher was terrified the dog would get caught in the middle of whatever danger had taken place.

He and Leora kept moving toward the location where the shooting took place. Before they were close enough to see anything, the vehicle sped away.

"They're leaving," he said as taillights hit the

dirt road and head off in the opposite direction from the station.

Fletcher tried not to lose hope. Molly appeared to be trained in on something near a group of trees. With dread in his limbs, Fletcher rushed to the dog's side and tried to hold it together. Spent shells and a massive amount of blood on the ground, followed by drag marks. There was little doubt in his mind. Ethan had been captured.

Though Leora wasn't a medical authority, so much blood loss usually represented a grave injury.

Her momentary burst of energy faded, yet stopping to rest wasn't an option. Ethan's and Tanner's lives were at stake.

"They'll no doubt take Ethan to wherever they're holding Tanner. We have a chance to save them both." Fletcher was trying to keep a positive outlook even though the situation was grave.

She struggled to catch her breath, drawing Fletcher's attention.

"I'm fine." *Please don't ask...* She wasn't ready to talk about it with him just yet. "Where do we go from here?"

"We stay out of sight and keep following the road. It's been a while since I've been through this area. There might be a house or someplace else where we can get help."

Moving forward was hard. Her body ached from exhaustion while her mind spun with conversations she'd had with Tanner in the past.

Had Tanner put his trust in someone involved in some type of illegal activity, and he'd found out about it? Maybe they'd threatened his life. That would explain her *bruder*'s nervous behavior prior to his disappearance. She wished Tanner had told her what had troubled him. Maybe she could have helped. Even prevented this from happening.

"Tanner told me some of the art he transported was quite valuable. Still, I can't believe someone he knew would do such a thing."

"Maybe these men have been doing it for a while, and Tanner somehow found out and—" He stopped short.

"What?" she asked, trying to understand the look on his face. "Fletcher?"

"And I don't know." He didn't want to tell her. "I guess I'm trying to understand how your *bruder* fits into all of this. Do you think it's possible Tanner might be involved in some way?"

Leora immediately rejected the idea. "No way." Yet a little niggling at the back of her mind reminded her of how Tanner had changed through the years. The deaths of their parents had affected them both greatly. Was it possible Tanner had inadvertently allowed himself to become enmeshed in some type of crime? She couldn't accept it. Not the boy she knew. Not her twin.

"Maybe he didn't have a choice in the matter," Fletcher said. "These men are ruthless, and they've proved they don't mind hurting anyone. They might have forced Tanner to do what they said or else."

If that was the case, then why hadn't Tanner told her that he was being threatened—or, if not her, Ethan.

"I guess it's possible," she begrudgingly admitted.

They'd lost the direction of the vehicle completely. Everything felt so helpless.

"Nothing unusual comes to mind in your conversations with your *bruder*?"

He was trying to understand every bit as much as she was, yet there wasn't anything... "I almost forgot."

"What?" Fletcher kept his attention on her face.

"Tanner had been talking a lot about the past and growing up in the Ruby Valley. How much he missed our life back there. Then, almost instantly, his demeanor changed suddenly.

He looked frightened. When I asked him what was wrong, he said if something were to happen to him, even if it looked like an accident, I shouldn't let them convince me it was. I should check it out."

As she recalled the bizarre conversation, her stomach clenched. Tanner had been trying to tell her something. She hadn't realized it at the time.

"He laughed and said he was only joking, and I shouldn't think anything about it because he was just tired."

Fletcher stopped walking. "He must have believed there was a chance someone would come after him—try and kill him. How long ago did this happen?"

Leora rubbed her forehead. "Maybe two months ago. And I spoke to him after this incident. He seemed happy, joking as if he'd never said any such thing." She wished she had questioned her *bruder* more—maybe gone to visit him—but she'd been in the middle of her chemo sessions and sick constantly.

"At this point, we don't know what's important and what isn't." Fletcher pointed to the dog. Molly had changed direction again and headed for a clearing.

The darkness continued to fade with the new day. At least it was easier to see if there were tracks but it would be harder for them to stay hidden. With so many men combing the woods, she couldn't help but believe they'd left several behind to find them. She and Fletcher were all that was standing between them and getting away with whatever they were planning.

Molly had picked up another scent.

It couldn't be Ethan's. "Maybe she's on Tanner." Leora sure hoped so. "She's a good tracker, isn't she?"

"One of the best. Sometimes animals are better than humans in these situations. At least they won't betray you." Fletcher's mouth thinned. She wondered if he was thinking about Catherine.

"I'm so sorry she broke your heart." Leora touched his arm. "But perhaps she wasn't the one *Gott* intended for you." Leora wasn't sure why she'd felt the need to add the last part.

His smile held bitterness. "I don't think I can let myself go down that road again. She and I have known each other since we were little. I grew up believing one day we'd be wed." He shook his head. "Catherine's betrayal completely destroyed my ability to trust. It made me realize I could count on my family and Ethan, but I no longer trusted anyone else."

As Leora looked into his blue eyes, her breath caught in her throat. This man had been beside her through some of the worst moments. He'd put his life on the line for her. He was a *gut* man—a handsome man. Someone she could trust her future with if only Leora believed she had one.

She struggled not to give in to emotions. After everything she and Fletcher had gone through, she was certain Tanner and Ethan were in the custody of these very dangerous men, and they had no idea where they were. "We have nothing, Fletcher. Nothing." Leora struggled not to give up. It seemed hopeless at this moment.

"Not nothing. The gas station owner should be arriving soon and…" His voice trailed off. His attention was focused on something in front of them.

"Fletcher?"

He gestured to a large clearing in the woods. Back-dropped against the trees was an enormous metal building. At first, Leora thought they'd circled around and were back at the logging company, but she promptly realized it was an entirely different structure.

"That building wasn't here the last time I came through here about a year ago," he told her in a shocked tone.

It appeared to be some type of warehouse. There was no name on the outside. Trees had been cleared away from near the structure.

There was a single door to one side and a couple of windows.

Leora stared up at it while a feeling she couldn't explain warned her to be careful.

"I don't see any sign of the vehicle. What is this place?" Fletcher carefully scanned the cleared space around the building. "Let's check it out, but we have to be careful. We don't know what might be waiting for us inside."

A shiver sped down her spine. Without warning, Molly charged straight for the warehouse before Fletcher could stop her. "She's definitely keyed on something."

Please let it be Tanner.

Leora's stomach twisted into knots as she stepped from their coverage. Her heartrate went ballistic when they reached the first window. She looked over Fletcher's shoulder. Rows and rows of shipping crates had been lined up inside the cavernous building.

"What on earth?" Leora whispered.

Fletcher tried the door. "It's locked." He looked up and froze. "Security cameras." Whoever owned the building could be watching them remotely—or worse, from inside.

"What if this building is connected to whatever those men are doing?" Leora's worst fear now was that they'd be captured before they could reach someone to help Ethan and Tanner.

"I sure hope not. It could be the owner placed the cameras there to keep whatever they've got stored inside safe, especially since the owner likely doesn't live around here. It stands to reason a business like this would have cameras around, considering its remoteness." What were they protecting?

Molly disappeared around the corner of the building, and they followed.

Once they reached the back of the structure, there were several sets of fresh tire tracks. A road had been cut out through the trees.

"Someone's been here recently." Fletcher noted two roll-up doors on docks used for loading and unloading trucks. One hadn't been closed completely.

A smaller door was flanked by a couple of windows. She and Fletcher glanced through the window. More crates and no sign of any type of office. "I don't see anyone inside. Where did Molly go?"

"Maybe she went through the opening."

Fletcher headed to the door. "We should be able to fit." He tucked his weapon inside his pocket and slipped under the opening. Leora did the same.

Once she got to her feet, Leora's eyes slowly adjusted to the dimness. The place appeared to be nothing but one big open space filled with shipping crates.

Rustling sounds came from somewhere inside.

"It's probably Molly," Fletcher said, clearly on edge. "There's a hallway over there. Why don't you wait here while I check it out?" He started to leave but she grabbed his arm.

"I'm coming with you. We've come this far together. We'll finish that way."

TEN

Several doors lined the hallway. The first one stood ajar. Fletcher tossed Leora a troubled look before pushing it the rest of the way open. Molly barked to give her location. If the dog was inside and there hadn't been a sound of a struggle, then chances were the room was vacant.

Fletcher tried the lights. The power was off. Another bad sign. He flicked on the flashlight. Molly ran toward them. The room was empty of any furniture. The floors were bare concrete.

"Let's keep checking." A search of the rest of the rooms proved more of the same and no sign of a phone. In the final room, a white powder was the only evidence anyone had been there at all.

He stared down at the substance. "I wonder if they're storing illegal drugs here?"

Leora knelt to examine the white powder. "Maybe we should try and look inside one of those crates."

Molly trotted into the main part of the warehouse and began investigating while Fletcher flashed the light around at the crates. He noticed something strange right away. One of the crates appeared to have been tampered with.

"Over there." Fletcher headed toward the crate. The lid was halfway off. He removed it and the packing material from on top.

A pallet of what appeared to be simple white crockery vases. Fletcher took one out and examined it. Had he been wrong about the drugs? "I don't get it. These are inexpensive vases you can get anywhere. Why would someone have a warehouse full of them?"

Leora looked past him into the crate. "Maybe these have nothing to do with the people chasing us. It could simply be a storage facility."

As much as Fletcher would like to believe it, he didn't. His attention went to Molly, who was sniffing at something on the floor.

Leora noticed the dog's behavior, as well. "She has something."

Fletcher reached the dog's side and eyed a wrapped cinnamon toothpick.

"Oh, no." Leora clasped her hand over her mouth. "Tanner loves those things. He smoked once and said chewing on them helped him break the habit."

"Tanner's been here at one time." Fletcher

picked up the toothpick and stuck it into his pocket. "He probably was the one who opened the crate."

Leora clutched her hands together. "Whatever's going on here, it's way beyond my understanding. Do you think the owner of the gas station has found the note yet?"

"Probably. They normally open early, as I recall." He looked around at the crate-filled space. "We should head back to the gas station and wait there for the sheriff." He started for the rear entrance when Leora grabbed onto a crate for support.

Right away, he could tell something was dreadfully wrong. Fletcher reached her side. "What's wrong?"

She closed her eyes and pulled in several breaths before answering. "I guess everything is finally catching up with me."

He helped her down to the floor and knelt beside her.

"I'll be *oke* in a moment, after I catch my breath." She assured him, but he wasn't so sure. Leora didn't look well.

He noticed a set of metal steps along one wall that led to another floor. "Stay here and rest. There's a floor above us. I'll take a look around."

Leora nodded without answering, and he hesitated. Her drawn features had him worried.

"Go—I will be fine," she said and managed a smile.

Fletcher slowly rose and headed up the steps, his weapon in his hand. Nothing about this place or what was stored in the crate made sense.

Fletcher went to the grimy window and looked out at the top of the trees in the woods. Miles and miles of woods, and no sign of anything to help them survive.

"*Gott,* I don't know what to do. Help me."

Staring out the window, he waited for an answer that didn't come.

Fletcher rubbed his hand across the back of his neck. They were wasting valuable time by staying here. As soon as Leora was able to travel again, they'd head back to the gas station. Hopefully, by the time they reached it, Sheriff Collins and his people would be looking for them.

He returned to Leora. She opened her eyes as he approached. He hated to dash the hopeful look on her face.

"There's nothing useful up there." He sat beside her. "How are you feeling?"

"Better." But she didn't look better.

"What's going on, Leora? This is more than exhaustion."

She stared at her clenched hands.

"You can trust me. I promise you can."

She slowly nodded. "You're right, there is."

Fear grabbed at his heart while all sorts of possibilities played through his head. None of them good.

"A few years back, I was diagnosed with breast cancer." Leora stopped and looked at him.

Nothing had prepared him for this. She waited for a response he couldn't give.

"Anyway, I had the lump removed and went through treatment." She grabbed a breath. "My doctor believed we'd caught it in time, and so I went back to my life. My work at the fabric shop—taking care of my aunt and uncle. Everything seemed to be fine. I felt good. At least, for a while."

"But it came back," he said.

She nodded. "*Jah*, it did. In the other breast and in the lymph nodes..." Her voice trailed off. He couldn't imagine the fear she'd gone through after receiving such a diagnosis.

"I had another surgery recently. My doctor once more believes they got it all. I finished the last of my treatment before I came here."

Fletcher reached for her hands and held them in his. Her fear for her *bruder*'s safety had been greater than her concern for her health. "I'm sorry you've had to go through this. I can't imagine how terrifying it was for you."

She smiled at his concern. "My aunt and

uncle are actually my great-aunt and -uncle, and they are getting up in years. They have been through so much. I couldn't burden them with what was going on with Tanner."

"You didn't tell them."

She nodded. "I couldn't. Uncle Tobias's health isn't the best and Aunt Marie is struggling with dementia. They don't need to be worried about Tanner or me." She sighed deeply. "And so, I told my boss I'd be gone for a week, and I asked her to check in on them. They're close," she said to his unasked question. "It will kill them if anything happens to Tanner. They adore him."

A strange thing to say. "I'm sure they feel the same about you."

She didn't answer for a moment. "They do." There was something she hadn't told him.

"What does your doctor say about your prognosis?"

"He tells me I have a good chance at having a normal life, but he'd said this before. You can't imagine how terrifying it was to hear the cancer had returned. I thought I would die." She shook her head. "I still might."

"You can't let fear control you, Leora. You deserve to be happy." His voice cracked under the weight of emotions he had no right to feel.

"That's sweet of you to say, but I haven't felt deserving of anything in a long time."

He could understand. Fletcher touched her cheek. They were both wounded souls. He leaned forward and touched his forehead to hers. "Don't give up on life, Leora. You have too much to offer."

A sob escaped and then she hugged him close. While he held her, something he'd buried so deep he'd thought it would never come back to life again proved him wrong. He pulled back and stared into her eyes before touching his lips to hers. Felt her tremble as she kissed him back.

He and Catherine had kissed only a few times, mostly a quick peck he'd thought had meant something. He'd been wrong. Kissing Leora was like being swept up into a whirlwind of emotions he hadn't thought himself capable of feeling.

Being on the run for their lives brought things into sharp focus. Normally, he wouldn't kiss a woman without really knowing her, but he wasn't sure if they'd survive what they were going through, and he did feel as if he knew Leora.

The kiss ended. Her wide eyes latched onto his. They stared at each other for the longest time before she smiled, and his heart lifted. Despite what they were going through, she gave him hope.

He cleared his throat. "Are you feeling up to

walking?" he asked because he needed something to say.

She seemed to understand. "I am. Resting helped." She glanced around to where Molly watched out the window. Always on guard. "We still have no idea where they've taken Ethan and Tanner. We know Ethan is hurt and in need of medical attention."

Molly whimpered at the mention of her owner's name and came over. Leora petted the dog. "She knows we're talking about Ethan."

Fletcher had never ceased to be amazed by how smart Molly was. "She and Ethan have been through a lot since he adopted her. She's loyal to him to death."

Leora leaned forward and looked into the dog's sad eyes. "We'll find him, Molly. We will."

"Let's get out of here. I want to reach the station before something else happens."

He rose and held out his hand to her. Leora took it, and he helped her to her feet.

Fletcher thought about how far they'd come on foot since being held hostage in the little storage shed. Leora had held up amazingly well considering everything she'd gone through.

The vases in the crate kept finding their way into his thoughts. Why would someone build a massive storage facility such as this if they were using it to store cheap vases? It didn't add up, but then, nothing about what they'd gone through made sense.

"Where do you think they'd take them?"

Leora's question interrupted his exhaustive thoughts. "At this point, I have no idea. There are plenty of places where someone can hide and never be found." He prayed they hadn't taken Ethan and Tanner out of the area.

"The sooner we reach the station, the better. I hope they haven't found whatever they believe Tanner has by now."

With Molly between them, they started for the back of the structure. Before Fletcher had the chance to unlock the door, a noise in the distance suddenly grabbed his attention. "Someone's coming." It sounded as if more than one vehicle was rumbling down the road toward them. "We have to get out of here." Fletcher prayed they hadn't been monitoring the security cameras. If so, they'd know he and Leora were in the building. They'd come looking.

Before they had the chance to leave the building, two container trucks rumbled from the shadows.

"Oh, no," Leora gasped. "What do we do?"

"This way." They ran toward the front of the building where he'd noticed the security cameras before. Fletcher peeked out the window. No sign of anyone yet. "We must hurry."

Molly stayed at their side as they reached the woods, but something had her troubled. The dog kept looking back at the structure.

Fletcher leaned close enough to whisper against Leora's ear. "We can't leave if there's a chance these men have Ethan and Tanner."

Leora didn't hesitate. "You're right. We can't."

Fletcher heard several men talking. They sounded as if they were far too close. He didn't want to put Leora in any more danger.

"Stay here with Molly. It will make less sound if I check it out alone." She didn't want to let go of his hand. He looked into her eyes and saw what he'd been looking to find all his life. What he'd thought he'd found in Catherine.

If only he'd met Leora at a different time.

Fletcher did his best to reassure her of something he didn't feel. "Don't worry. I'll be back soon."

She slowly let him go. He held onto her gaze for a long moment, memorizing every inch of her pretty face, before turning away. Fletcher kept a tight grip on the weapon in his hand and prayed he wouldn't have to use it. He slowly edged toward the trucks. The back of the warehouse was visible through the trees. The two trucks were parked near the loading docks. The roll-up doors were both opened. Men were loading the crates into the trucks.

Who were these men, and what were they storing here? One of the men appeared to look right at him, and Fletcher quickly ducked back. His foot connected with a twig. His eyes widened, and he prayed he hadn't sealed both his and Leora's fate.

Someone was coming. Leora ducked out of sight while grabbing Molly's collar to keep her from charging.

With her heart threatening to explode from her chest, she peeked around the edge of the tree and saw Fletcher hurrying her way. Leora quickly left her hiding place. Fletcher spotted her and grasped her arm. He didn't slow down.

"Did you figure out who they are?" she asked as they hurried through the trees.

"*Nay*, but they're armed to the teeth, and they're moving the crates from the building. Whatever they're up to, it isn't *gut*." Molly stopped behind them and sniffed the air.

Leora glanced over her shoulder in alarm as the dog appeared to be watching the building. "She's on to something."

Before Fletcher could get the dog's attention, Molly broke for the building. Fletcher grabbed for her, but she was already out of reach.

The dog suddenly barked loudly. Alerting the men to their presence.

A second later, a shot rang out. Molly whimpered loudly. Leora bit her bottom lip to hold back a scream.

Please let her be oke.

"Fletcher, we can't leave her." She couldn't think about deserting Molly after all she'd done to protect them.

"We don't have a choice. They'll know the dog isn't here by herself. We have to keep going." Fletcher took hold of her hand and forced her out of her daze. Moving as fast as they could while still keeping their location secret, they headed away from the building.

After some time, Fletcher stopped abruptly. "Did you hear something?"

She listened, but all she heard was the sound of her own heartbeat. "I don't hear anything."

"We should be far enough away to start heading for the station." As they continued walking at a fast pace, Leora caught glimpses of the building through the trees. Another truck was coming up the road. She pointed to the vehicle. Both she and Fletcher stopped.

The SUV stopped beside one of the trucks.

A man and woman exited the vehicle.

"That's Jade. I recognize her from the sink hole. She wasn't wearing a mask."

Leora must have made some sound because Fletcher's attention went to her.

"Do you recognize that man?"

She did. Leora had seen the man's face on the website Tanner showed her on his phone. He'd been so proud to be part of the team.

"That's Zeke Bowman. Tanner's former boss."

Fletcher's head jerked toward the new man. "Why would Tanner's boss be here with Jade? He's the one in charge? She spoke about having to check with someone else."

Leora tried to make sense of what was before her. Tanner's boss had taken him hostage, along with Ethan. Why would Bowman kidnap her *bruder*?

"I don't understand any of this," she whispered desperately.

"I agree, but we can't help either Ethan or Tanner by getting ourselves caught. And we sure can't figure this out ourselves. We have to get to the station, Leora. It's the only way to save them."

She slowly nodded. "You're right. I know you're right."

Before she could take a single step, someone was dragged from the SUV. The person had been beaten. They were in such bad shape she couldn't tell if it was her *bruder* or Ethan. "What do we do?"

The injured man was forced inside the ware-house.

"Let's go back to the front of the building and see if we can figure out where they'll take him. Maybe there's a chance we can make it inside and get to him before they spot us." He looked her in the eye. "It's dangerous, Leora. Maybe you should stay here and wait. If I don't return in a few minutes, keep going this way." He pointed in the direction they'd been heading.

"*Nay*, Fletcher." Her voice broke. She couldn't leave him here with these dangerous men.

"If they capture me, at least you will be able to get away. Reach the station and get the sher-iff."

She understood, but it was still hard letting him go. She clutched his hand. "Be careful. Please don't take any risks. I-I don't want to lose you."

He looked deep into her eyes before slowly nodding. "If I'm not back in ten minutes, get out of here. Promise me you will."

"I promise."

"Stay out of sight, and remember what I told you. Ten minutes. No longer."

Tears she couldn't stop blinded her for a moment. Would she lose him, too?

Fletcher ran his hand across her cheek. She leaned into it, her eyes holding his. As he turned and left her, she watched him disappear through the trees and prayed he would be safe, and that this nightmare would end soon.

Leora counted off each second in her head while keeping her attention on the SUV. Jade was there by herself now. The man had gone inside with the others. Jade appeared to keep a close watch on the building while she typed something on her phone.

A second later, the man returned, and she shoved her phone back into her pocket. Leora listened closely, but it was impossible to catch more than a few random words. As she leaned in closer, she caught a name that sent fear throughout her body. They'd mentioned Tanner. The man seemed to indicate he would talk soon enough.

What had they done to her *bruder*?

She tried to look in the direction Fletcher had disappeared, but she couldn't see anything. Was he safe?

Ten minutes came and went. Still, Leora hesitated. She hated leaving Fletcher here alone. While she struggled with her conscience, two quick pops from a weapon came from the direction Fletcher had gone. Her heart clenched. She couldn't leave. Not with Fletcher in danger.

With her mind made up, Leora ran toward the sound of the shots. As she drew near, she spotted Fletcher crouching behind a tree. He whirled around, the weapon aimed at her. Leora stopped short.

"Get down, Leora. They know we're here." He fired a couple of times to cover her as she practically dove for him.

Leora righted herself and got as close to Fletcher as she could.

"How do they know?"

"The security cameras. I heard one of the men mention they'd seen us on the cameras. We can't stay here."

She clutched his arm before he could take a single step. "We can't leave him behind."

"If they capture us, we won't be able to help anyone." He rose and pulled her up beside him.

Before they had the chance to move, a noise nearby caught her attention. She whipped toward it in time to see several men rush their way. Something hard slammed against her temple.

"Leora." Fletcher yelled her name.

Her legs deserted her. Leora barely registered Fletcher yelling. Soon, the sounds of a struggle became muffled. She hit the ground hard and fell to her side. Something landed close by. She struggled to open her eyes. Fletcher. His eyes were closed.

"No," she mumbled, the word garbled. Her

fingers stretched out across the soggy ground toward him, but she couldn't reach him. A tear slipped from her eye when someone hauled her up and started dragging her toward the building. She tried to keep sight of Fletcher.

"No, don't leave him." Leora wasn't sure she'd actually said the words aloud.

"Get her quiet," someone said.

"No, please," she begged, but her captors were heartless. Another blow struck the side of her head, and she screamed as the darkness closed in to be replaced with nothingness.

ELEVEN

His head throbbed mercilessly. Opening his eyes was impossible. Fletcher shifted slightly. Pain splintered through his body. He went to move his arms but they were secured behind him.

Fletcher tried again with the same result.

Open your eyes!

Fletcher forced them open. Nothing but blurred images first appeared. He struggled to recall what had happened.

He and Leora had been attacked. Someone had struck Leora. Before he could get to her aide, he'd been knocked out.

After blinking several times, the world came into focus. He was back inside the warehouse. All the crates were now gone. The space was empty. Fletcher craned his neck enough to be able to see that he'd been secured to a beam running from the floor to the ceiling.

Someone moaned beside him. He turned his

head. Leora was restrained beside him. She was alive.

He glanced around the cavernous space and realized no one was there. Had the men who'd attacked them left? He couldn't believe they would leave witnesses behind. After all, they'd both seen their faces.

"Leora," he said as quietly as possible. "Leora, wake up."

She slowly opened her eyes and looked at him with sheer terror. "What happened?" Her voice was little more than a whisper.

"We were knocked unconscious. We're in the building again."

Her eyes widened as she looked around. "Where are all those containers?"

He shook his head and winced. "They've transferred them all into the trucks."

"Do you think they've left?"

He didn't. "They can't afford to leave us here alive."

The truth dawned in her eyes. "Do you still have your knife?"

He'd tucked the weapon into his boot. His legs were stretched out in front of him. He could no longer feel the knife against his foot. "They must have searched me while I was unconscious and found it." That meant he and Leora would have to find a way to work their restraints free.

He stretched his fingers out and was able to form an idea of what type of restraint had been used. "They're zip ties." There would be no way to work the ties loose.

From where they sat, they were facing the roll-up doors, which were now closed. He listened and could hear voices. He couldn't tell how many.

"Help me look for a nail or anything sharp we can use to work our restraints free."

Fletcher ignored the pain shooting from the injury in his head and searched around. The massive wooden beams were smooth. There would be no need for nails unless something had been hung there.

He turned the other way so he could see how they each were bound. Leora had been secured beneath his restraints.

"I'm going to see if I can stand up and get some traction to break the ties. If I can move them back and forth against the edge of the beam, it might work. Keep watch for me." He pulled his knees against his chest, then raised his arms as far as he could reach and heaved his body up and into a squatting position. His shoulder throbbed along with the ankle. The pain from his injured head shot through him, causing his stomach to heave. He stopped and closed his eyes while waves of nausea washed over him.

"Are you *oke*?" Leora asked, seeing his struggle.

"I need a moment." Unfortunately, they didn't have a lot of those. Getting his hands free was only the beginning. When his stomach stopped roiling, he lifted his arms higher and rose to his full height. With his legs beneath him, he felt somewhat more able to maneuver his hands into a better position to work on the restraints.

"Fletcher," Leora murmured, pulling his attention from the task.

"What is it? Is someone coming?"

He looked down and could see she wasn't looking at the doors but at something behind him. The fear on her face scared him. Fletcher edged around the beam until he could see what had her attention. He barely recognized it as a person and probably wouldn't have thought so if he didn't recognize the camo jacket. "That's Ethan." And he wasn't moving.

"Is he…?"

Fletcher swallowed deeply. He couldn't continue what was needed if he let himself think about his friend as dead. Anger boiled inside him. These men had hurt his friend, hurt Leora's *bruder*, all for their own gain? For whatever they had hidden inside those crates.

He worked harder, angrier. *Help me*, Gott. *I can't let my friend die. I can't let Leora down.*

"Fletcher, someone's coming."

The words sent a wave of fear through his body. A second later, he heard the footsteps and sank down to the floor beside her.

"What do we do?" she whispered with panic in her tone.

"Whatever it takes to stay alive."

The door flew open. Half a dozen armed men stepped into the warehouse. They fanned around the door as if to make way for someone else. Who were they waiting for?

Fletcher didn't have to wait long to find out. Two people entered the room. Jade and the man Leora had identified as Zeke Bowman.

Bowman purposefully strode toward Leora while Jade kept up with him.

Bowman stopped in front of Leora and looked down at her with disgust. "You know who I am?"

Fletcher could feel Leora's trembling from where he sat. He squeezed her finger with his.

"You're Zeke Bowman, Tanner's boss."

The man continued to eye her for a long moment. "Former boss. Your brother stole something from me, and I want it back."

Leora shrank against the post when Bowman leaned in close. "I want it now."

"I-I don't know what you are talking about. I've already told your men as much."

Bowman got a few inches from her face. "You're lying. He told you something when he came to see you."

They'd been watching Tanner for some time. Had probably been suspicious of him for a while. They'd known he'd visited Leora.

"Leave her alone. She's told you already she doesn't know anything."

Bowman's angry eyes slanted to Fletcher. "Keep your mouth shut. You are of no benefit to us." Anger flashed down deep in Bowman's eyes before his attention returned to Leora. "Well?"

"I told you, I don't know anything."

This wasn't the answer Bowman wanted. "Bring him in," he ordered Jade.

She turned to one of the men lined up near the door. "Well, you heard him. Go get him."

Bowman slowly smiled as if satisfied he'd frightened Leora.

Fletcher's gut twisted with dread as two of the men returned with a badly beaten man between them.

"Tanner!" Leora exclaimed. Tears filled her eyes and fell freely.

Fletcher watched in horror as her *bruder* was dragged into the room and closer to where they were bound.

The two dropped Tanner. He wasn't moving.

"Tanner. Oh, Tanner," Leora sobbed his name. "What did you do to him?" she yelled at Bowman.

A smile curled Bowman's lip. "You can save him by telling me where the stuff is hidden."

"I can't tell you what I don't know," she shouted in a frantic voice.

Bowman glanced at one of the men, who kicked Tanner hard.

"No!" Leora shrieked when her brother groaned.

"Last chance. You can end his pain by telling me where it's hidden."

"Please, don't hurt him. I don't know what you're talking about, but my *bruder* wouldn't have done whatever you think he's done. Please, let us go."

Bowman motioned to the two men who then grabbed Tanner's arms and started for the door.

"No! Let him go," Leora cried, but it was no use. Tanner was taken from the building.

"Too bad. I kind of liked him until he became a liability." Bowman glanced past them to where Ethan was so quiet. "Like your friend there."

Once more, anger rose inside Fletcher as he watched Bowman grin nastily.

"I'll give you a little time to think about what you're risking. Tanner won't last long where he's going. I suggest you make up your mind how important your brother is to you before it's too late." With those chilling words, Bowman and his group left the warehouse. As Jade started to close the door, she glanced back at them. Something in her eyes made Fletcher wonder if she was as "on board" with Bowman's tactics as she was pretending to be.

The door slammed shut. Beside him, Leora wept. Fletcher tried to think of something to say to ease her pain, but the reality was that time was running out for them and for Tanner.

He couldn't look behind him because he was so certain Ethan was dead already.

"We have to keep trying, Leora. We can't give up. By now, Sheriff Collins will have arrived at the station, and he and his people will be looking for us."

He wished he could take her in his arms and comfort her. Instead, he entwined her pinky finger with his and squeezed it.

She slowly looked at him. "I can't let him die. He's my *bruder*."

Fletcher's heart broke for her. "Help is coming. We have to stay alive long enough for them to reach us."

She released a shuddering breath. "I know you're right."

He forced a smile. "I'm going to try again to get my restraints off." He leaned closer. "Don't give up, Leora. Tanner needs you to keep fighting. I need you to keep fighting. For us." And he did. *Gott* had brought them together, and he didn't want to lose her or this second chance at happiness. Not like this. Not to these dangerous men.

"Ethan, can you hear me?" Leora called out to her friend. There was no response. She stared at his limp frame and willed him to stir. "He hasn't moved in a very long time."

"I know. I'll keep working on getting the restraints free," Fletcher told her.

She slowly pulled her gaze away from Ethan. But what about Tanner? The image of her beaten *bruder* made her want to cry out in sheer helplessness.

Fletcher rose once more and began working the ties on his wrists back and forth. Leora couldn't sit back and let him do everything. She got her feet under her and stood beside him. "We both must free our hands," she said in a way of an answer to his questioning look.

Fletcher smiled and continued to work. She studied what he was doing before repeating the effort.

While she worked, Leora watched the door. "What do you think they're up to?"

Fletcher looked over at her. "It has something

to do with those vases, and I'm guessing Tanner figured it out. They can't let whatever information he may have taken get out to the public. Whatever it is will be enough to land Bowman and his thugs in jail. Probably for a long time. They'll do anything to keep this from happening."

"Even murder?" she asked because nothing she could even come close to imagining would warrant what they were doing.

He shook his head. "I know it's hard to imagine. At one time, I felt the same way."

She looked at him curiously. "You've been through something like this before?"

He stopped to reposition his wrists before answering. "I have. Some very bad men came into our community on several different occasions. They did terrible things and hurt people I love."

Her eyes widened as she watched his face. "I'm sorry. I had no idea."

Fletcher swallowed. "It was hard, but you have been a victim, too."

He meant what had happened to her family, but he didn't know her involvement.

Fletcher's restraints snapped free. His huge eyes found hers. "I'll help you get yours off."

"No—Ethan needs you. I'll keep working on mine."

She sawed harder while alternately watching the door and Fletcher.

Fletcher knelt beside Ethan and checked for a pulse. "He's alive," he exclaimed. "But he's been shot a couple of times." Fletcher gently rolled Ethan over onto his back. A large bloodstain covered the front of Ethan's shirt. "He's in bad shape, Leora. He needs a hospital."

Out of the corner of her eye, Leora spotted something moving. She jerked toward it and realized it was Molly. The dog had blood on her fur.

Molly trotted over to Ethan and licked his face.

Fletcher balled his coat up against Ethan's wound and quickly examined the dog. "She has an injury, which appears she may have been grazed by a bullet." He got the dog's attention. "Molly, go home. I need you to go home."

The dog didn't want to leave her owner, but she obeyed Fletcher's command and headed out the open door at the front of the building.

"It's a longshot. We're quite some distance from the community, but if Sheriff Collins's people go to Ethan's place, I'm hoping Molly can lead them to our location. How are you coming with the restraints?"

"I'm trying, but it isn't easy. Maybe you should go without me."

"That's not going to happen." He rejected the idea immediately. "I'm not leaving you behind with these guys."

"Fletcher, it might be our only chance. Ethan needs help."

He rose and came over to her. "I'm not leaving you." He held her gaze, and her heart tumbled.

"Let me help you." He took her wrists and gently began working them back and forth. "You're close."

Leora prayed Molly would reach someone who could assist, or the note at the station would bring the sheriff's people into the woods.

Her restraints snapped free.

Ethan moaned and they hurried to his side.

He suddenly opened his eyes and stared at them. "How did you find me?" He croaked the words out.

"Molly," Fletcher explained about running into the animal near Sam's place.

Ethan coughed violently and grabbed his waist. "Where's Tanner?"

"These men have him." Fletcher told him what happened. "Leora Mast is here with me. She came to West Kootenai, looking for you when you couldn't reach you by phone. I'm going to help you to your feet. We have to get out of here."

Ethan slowly nodded, his attention on Leora. "It's good to put a face to a name, but I hate that it's under these circumstances, Leora. I can't believe you came here after everything you've gone through." She'd told Ethan about her cancer. A testament to the strength of their friendship despite never having met in person.

Leora squeezed his arm. "Of course, I came. I wanted to help you and my *bruder*."

Fletcher wrapped his arm around Ethan's waist, and he flinched. "I'm sorry, buddy." Fletcher struggled to get them both up while Ethan clamped down on his bottom lip to keep from screaming in pain.

"I know it hurts." Once they were standing, Fletcher took a second to let Ethan rest before they started toward the front entrance. "Leora, you will have to be my eyes. Can you check and see if there are men stationed near the front?"

She hurried ahead of them and looked through the windows facing out. "I don't see anyone. Let me check outside."

Leora stepped from the building, half expecting to be shot. When nothing happened, she checked around the front. Where was everyone?

She went back inside. "There's no one out front. We'd better hurry before they come back." She held the door open while Fletcher assisted Ethan outside. Her heart tattooed a frantic beat.

Even if Molly reached someone, it could be hours, if not longer, before help reached them. And it might take just as long before Sheriff Collins found their exact location. They didn't have that much time to spare.

Moving a severely injured man was difficult, and Fletcher was struggling. She stepped to the opposite side of Ethan and put her arm around his waist. Her friend appeared to be drifting in and out of consciousness. His head rolled backward as his full weight slumped against her. Leora stumbled and almost dropped to her knees.

"Hold on." Fletcher stopped and adjusted his hold to take on more of Ethan's weight. Ethan bellowed when Fletcher accidently contacted the injury. He immediately passed out from the pain.

"There's no way they didn't hear." Leora glanced behind them, expecting the door to burst wide and armed men to start firing.

"We have to reach those woods and get out of the open." She and Fletcher ran as fast as they could with the unconscious Ethan between them.

Before they reached the first of the trees, her worst fear was realized. The door slammed against the wall. Multiple men emerged from the building.

"Over there. Don't let them get away." Zeke Bowman had spotted them.

"Hurry, Leora." Fletcher took on Ethan's full weight and kept heading for the woods.

Behind her, shots rang out all around them. One whizzed past Leora's face and grazed her cheek. She screamed. Another shot struck Fletcher's arm. He staggered. Lost his footing and fell with Ethan.

"No." She stumbled and hit the ground.

Fletcher spotted her. "Stay down, Leora."

The words barely registered when another shot rang in her ears. Something hot burrowed deep into her calf. She shouted and stumbled forward. Leora tried to catch herself but couldn't. She hit the ground hard.

"Leora." Fletcher called out her name.

She began crawling toward the sound of his voice. Before she could reach him, two armed men grabbed her arms and hauled her up.

"No, please."

They didn't listen. They dragged her along between them. Leora looked over her shoulder in time to see two more men dragging Fletcher, while others bent over Ethan.

She craned her neck as she was forced into the building. What were they going to do with Ethan? She was terrified they'd kill him.

Her eyes filled with tears once more. She

couldn't have imagined what would happen when she'd left her home in Colorado to come and seek out Ethan. Because of her, he and Fletcher might die.

The two men slung her down near the beam she'd been tied to before.

"You really should have told the truth," Bowman said nastily as he watched them secure her hands behind her. "Tighter. I don't want them getting loose again."

He stood back and watched as one of the men yanked the restraints mercilessly around her wrists. She winced and bit her bottom lip to keep from crying out and giving Bowman the satisfaction of seeing her pain.

Once her hands were secured, he inspected the man's work. "Good. That should keep her in place." His gaze shifted toward the door. Two men hauled Fletcher over and dumped him near a second beam. They secured Fletcher's hands in the same fashion as Leora's. Ethan was also dragged in but was left unconscious near the front door. Leora couldn't look at him without crying. They believed he no longer posed a threat.

Bowman knelt in front of her and stared at her injured leg. "Looks like it hurts. I could take care of it, but why would I? You haven't been exactly forthcoming." He touched her leg close to the injury and smiled when she gritted her teeth to keep from showing the pain. Bowman rose. "We'll be back soon. This is your last time to help your brother. If you want to keep him alive, I suggest you cooperate." Bowman motioned to his men and strode through the door with them following him outside.

"How bad is it?" Fletcher asked with urgency the second they were gone.

"I don't know." She adjusted her leg to where her foot was flat on the ground and tried to put some weight on it. The pain was excruciating. "I can't stand." Her fearful gaze found him. "Fletcher, they're going to kill us. Can you get your hands free?"

He tried to wiggle his wrists enough to gain leverage, but the restraints were too tight. "I can't even budge them." He turned his head her way. "The sheriff is coming. I know he is."

It would be a longshot if they were still alive when the sheriff arrived.

"We have to hold on," he softly assured her.

Leora did her best not to fall apart. "You're right. Help will be here soon." But she didn't believe it.

She tried her wrists without any real hope. Bowman had made sure they'd both been secured tight enough so there would be no repeat of what had happened before.

Leora closed her eyes and prayed silently, *Help us, please,* Gott. *We can't do this without You.*

She glanced over to where Fletcher watched her. He looked so exhausted. Her heart broke. He was innocent in all of this. As was Ethan. Whatever Tanner had gotten involved in had hurt so many people.

"Hey, it's going to be *oke,*" Fletcher told her. "This isn't the end of us. You and I will get through this. We'll save Ethan and your *bruder* and then..."

He stopped, and her heart soared at the tenderness she saw in his eyes. "I want to believe that. I don't want this to be the end of us, either."

"It won't be," he said earnestly, holding her gaze. She didn't want to look away—even when the door opened and armed men marched inside. She embraced his stare and drew comfort in the strength she saw in him.

TWELVE

"Last chance, Tanner."

Fletcher watched in horror as Bowman motioned to the man holding Leora's brother. Tanner was forced over to where Bowman stood near Leora.

Bowman grabbed Tanner's face and forced him to look at Leora. "You see this? This is all your fault."

Tanner's gaze latched with his sister's. The pain on his face was devastating. "I'm so sorry."

Bowman didn't let go. "You should be. Because you took something which wasn't yours, your sister and these two men have been pulled into your problem." Bowman released Tanner and stepped closer to Leora. With his eyes on Tanner still, he directed Jade over to his side.

"How could you do this, Jade?" Tanner asked incredulously.

Tanner knew Jade. How?

"Keep quiet," Jade ordered.

Tanner jerked his head back as if she'd struck him.

"Do it," Bowman ordered Jade.

She held a gun in her hand and, kneeling beside Leora, placed the barrel against her temple.

"No," Fletcher yelled. Jade's attention switched to Fletcher. There was something in her eyes he couldn't define. She didn't have the appearance of a hardcore killer, but then he didn't really know what was in her heart.

Leora's frightened eyes held to her *bruder*'s.

"What's it going to be?" Bowman demanded. "Save your secrets or your sister."

There were tears in Tanner's eyes.

When he didn't respond, Bowman nodded to Jade. "Do it."

The woman pulled the trigger back on the weapon.

"No! Don't hurt her," Tanner yelled frantically.

Jade brought the weapon away from Leora's temple.

"I'll tell you where it's hidden. Please don't hurt her."

Bowman smiled slowly. "Glad to hear you've come to your senses. Bring him with us."

Jade rose and followed Bowman and his men from the building.

Fletcher blew out a long breath. "That was too close."

Leora turned her head toward him. "Once they get back whatever it is Tanner took, we'll be dead."

Her pain was his. But she was right. Their time was numbered.

By now, several hours had passed since they'd left the note. He believed Sheriff Collins was searching for them. Would he find them too late?

Fletcher looked behind him to where Ethan remained far too still.

He couldn't lose his friend. And he couldn't lose Leora. He'd given up on love. Thought he was one of those men who was meant to be alone. Work was the only thing to keep him going. Many times, he and Ethan would talk long into the night about their lives. Ethan had loved his wife so much, and then she'd died. Ethan still felt the loss. Fletcher had thought he'd felt the same for Catherine.

Outside, a gunshot cracked, breaking the silence. Leora jumped. "Do you think they killed Tanner?"

Though it was Fletcher's first thought, he didn't want her to give up hope. "No way. Why would they shoot him until Bowman is certain Tanner is telling the truth?"

"What do you mean?" she asked and forced her attention from the direction of the shot.

"I'm guessing Tanner hid whatever they're looking for near your home in Colorado. They'll have to have someone go there and get it. They can't kill him until they know for certain he isn't lying."

She slowly nodded. "You're right. It will take a while. There's hope." She smiled despite the grave situation.

He returned her smile. "How's your leg?"

Leora glanced down at the gunshot wound. "It hurts, but with everything else going on, it's the least of my concerns. What about you?"

He'd been shot, but the bullet had gone straight through. "Little more than a graze."

He shifted his arm around. The pain was there, but nothing compared to what she'd suffered.

"How does Tanner know Jade?" Fletcher remembered what Tanner had said.

Leora shook her head. "I wish I knew."

He glanced around the space for something to use to their benefit while mentally taking stock of what he had on his person. His suspenders might work as a weapon, but with his hands tied behind him, he couldn't get them loose. Getting his hands free was critical.

Fletcher kept his attention on the door. Think! There had to be a way. This couldn't be the end.

His thoughts returned to Ethan. Fletcher had seen the damage done by the bullet. Ethan needed help right away. It was up to him to get it for him.

Something shiny caught his eye. He leaned forward as far as he could and realized it was a nail. If he could stretch out his foot far enough to reach it, he might be able to kick it close to his hands.

"Do you see it?" Fletcher indicated the nail.

"I do." The hope on her face felt like a weight had settled on his shoulders. He couldn't let her down.

"I'm going to push it closer."

Fletcher scooched around so he faced the nail. Even the slightest movement hurt like crazy, but he ignored the pain.

He got as low as possible before stretching out his leg. Not quite. The self-doubt he'd struggled with since Catherine's rejection reared its ugly head. He'd never make it in time. Fletcher shoved the negative thoughts back and shifted himself lower until he was almost lying flat on the floor.

You can do this.

Once more, he extended his leg. This time

the tip of his boot touched the nail. His heart leaped to his throat.

"I've got it." He looked at Leora and grinned.

"Oh, thank goodness."

Fletcher slowly inched the nail closer. He lost control once, and the nail rolled away. "No..." Frustration rose again. He pulled in a couple of breaths to steady himself before Fletcher stretched his leg toward the metal object and eased it to him. The nail rolled away several times, and he was forced to start over.

Little by little, he inched the nail forward until he was able to sit up. He nudged the nail closer to his fingers.

"Can you get it into your hand?"

Fletcher did his best to study the situation, though it was difficult with his hands behind his back. "I sure hope so." He kept careful watch on the door before lowering his wrists as close as possible to the floor. He strained to see the nail. Just out of reach.

"Ugh, almost." Fletcher circled his foot around, coaxed the nail a little closer, and tried again. His index finger touched the head of the nail. When it slipped a little, he stopped and let his fingers hover above it. He could feel them trembling. One false move and their only chance to free themselves would roll out of reach.

Fletcher gathered himself and tried again.

This time he was able to fold it into his hand. "I've got it." He never thought he'd be so happy to hold a nail.

"Oh, wonderful…" Fletcher glanced her way. She had slumped against the beam. Between the effects of chemo and being shot, she was fading fast.

"Hang on, Leora. Please, hang on."

She smiled faintly.

Fletcher clasped the nail between his fingers and adjusted it around until the sharp point faced out. Now, all he had to do was work it against the zip ties when he could barely wiggle his wrists.

Hopelessness washed over him. He fought to keep it at bay. He couldn't give up. Too many people were counting on him.

He gripped the nail tight and jabbed at the plastic restraint. The nail's point bounced off several times. Finally, he used enough force for it to stick into the heavy plastic ties. Fletcher dug into the material as deep as he could, but the restraints didn't snap.

"Fletcher, someone's coming."

Leora's words sent terror through him. If their captors found the nail, his only chance of breaking the restraints would be gone. Fletcher continued to jab at the plastic while his eyes darted to the entrance.

Multiple footsteps appeared to be right outside. He and Leora were out of time.

Near the loading docks, the door flew open and slammed against the wall hard.

Zeke Bowman and his goons filed into the warehouse. Fletcher noticed Jade hung back near the door.

Right away, Fletcher could tell something had happened.

Bowman lost no time filling them in. "Your brother lied." His face became flushed with anger. "He told us he hid the information in a storage unit, but he lied." Was it Fletcher's imagination or was Bowman becoming more unstable? He jerked his weapon from the waist of his jeans and pointed it at Leora's face. "Last chance. Where did your brother hide the stuff?"

Leora shrank away from the weapon, shaking her head repeatedly. "I can't help you with what I don't know. I told you, I have no idea what you are talking about."

Bowman brought the gun dangerously closer before finally dropping it to his side. "Fine, you don't want to talk…well, it really doesn't matter. If you and your brother are dead, you can't rat us out."

Leora's eyes widened and Bowman slowly grinned. "That's right. I've dealt with Tanner already in a way fitting for him. Now, it's your turn."

"No." The word jerked from her lips.

Bowman ignored Leora and swung back to his people. He searched the faces of those around him. "Kill them." Bowman turned his smug expression on Fletcher. "All of them."

"I'll handle it." Jade stepped forward, her confident gaze on her boss's face.

Bowman eyed her for a long moment. "Good. Do it quickly. We have to get out of here soon, otherwise the shipment will be late and that won't be good for us."

Jade pulled out her weapon and started toward them.

"Let's go, people. Get the trucks ready to leave immediately." Bowman strode from the building, followed by the rest of his thugs.

As soon as the door closed, Jade stepped in front of Fletcher, the gun in her hand. She quickly tucked it behind her back, pulled a knife from her jeans' pocket, and knelt beside Fletcher.

"My name is Jade Powell, and I'm an FBI agent. I've been working undercover in Bowman's organization." She glanced behind her as if expecting Bowman to return. "There's not much time. I have to find Tanner. Bowman talked about burying him somewhere on the property. I couldn't stop him. Tanner will die if I can't get to him in time." She cut Fletcher's restraints. "Can you stand?"

Fletcher nodded. "I'm able. Leora is in bad shape, though."

Jade hurried to Leora and examined her leg while keeping a careful eye on the door. "It was a clean shot, Leora, which means the bullet exited your leg." She cut Leora's restraints and then ripped off the bottom of her shirt to make a tourniquet while she continued to stare at Leora as if she recognized her.

Once she'd finished, Jade rushed to Ethan and examined his injuries. "He's in bad shape." Her voice sounded unsteady, as if she and Ethan knew each other. "I need you to keep pressure on his abdomen to stop the bleeding." Jade brought out some bandages from her jacket pocket and placed one against Ethan's injury.

Fletcher hurried to his friend and knelt beside Jade. He took over putting pressure on the wound from her.

"I'm sorry I have to go, but help is coming. Stay here. Whatever you hear outside, don't leave the building."

She took out her weapon and fired off one shot, then another, and a third. Jade handed Fletcher a second gun. "Just in case." She dug in her jeans' pocket and pulled out a cell phone. "I called for backup, but we changed our location so they may not find us in time. Reach Sheriff Collins, and make sure he knows to come to this location. Tell him to send medical help for Ethan and Tanner, and from the looks of it, both of you could use some assistance." She glanced at Ethan. "Take care of him. Don't let him die."

With a final glance at Leora, Jade crossed to the door and stepped outside.

While keeping pressure on Ethan's injury, Fletcher dialed 9-1-1.

The familiar dispatcher's voice was a welcomed relief. Fletcher didn't waste time identifying himself. "I need to speak with Sheriff Collins." He told the woman what he knew.

"Fletcher, Sheriff Collins and his deputies, along with the FBI, are on their way. Thank you for giving us your updated location. I'll pass it along to the team. Are you safe?"

Fletcher had no idea. "I hope so. We're inside a building, but we have a severely injured man and a woman who has been shot in the leg. I sustained a minor gunshot wound. There's a missing man, and we have a federal agent here on site. She could be in danger."

"Agent Jade Powell." The dispatcher knew about Jade. "It is our understanding Ethan's former soldier, Tanner Mast, is there, as well."

"That's correct. He's the one who's missing."

A noise nearby had him jerking toward it, his nerves shot. Leora slowly hobbled his way. He breathed out a sigh of relief.

"Stay safe. Help is on the way. Please leave this line open in case we need to track your location."

Fletcher set the phone down. Blood had soaked through the bandage. He opened another bandage and replaced the soiled one.

Leora carefully lowered herself to the floor beside Ethan. She indicated Ethan's shoulder wound. Blood trickled from where he'd been shot earlier. "It doesn't appear too serious."

Fletcher nodded. Right now, the bullet wound in Ethan's abdomen was their primary concern. "I never thought I'd say a bullet wound wasn't serious, but in light of what Ethan has going on, I'd say my shoulder is the least of our worries."

Outside, a rash of gunshots pulled Fletcher's attention away from his injured friend.

"Tanner." Leora's gaze locked with his. "What if Jade couldn't get to him in time? Or they killed her before…" She drew in a breath. "Fletcher, he might die."

"Take over for me with Ethan. I'm going to see if I can find out what's happening." Leora placed her hands on the bandage. Fletcher rose unsteadily and headed for the window at the back of the building near the roll-up doors.

Before he reached it, another round of shots sounded far too close. Fletcher hit the floor. Several bullets sprayed across the side of the warehouse.

Leora leaned over Ethan to protect him until the shooting stopped. "Fletcher?"

"I'm *oke*." He hopped to his feet. "I don't hear anything." The window he'd been heading toward was now shattered. Rain and cold air blew through the building.

Ethan moaned softly, drawing Leora's attention back to her friend. He opened his eyes. When he spotted Leora, he tried to sit up.

"Don't try to move. Help is on the way."

"What happened?" His voice sounded so weak. "Where's Tanner?" Once more, he tried to sit up, but Leora stopped him.

Gunfire sounded as if it were coming from all directions. Leora instinctively covered Ethan. "Jade is going to find Tanner. He'll be *oke*." And he would be. *Gott* wouldn't take her *bruder*. Not like this. Not when they'd fought so hard to find him.

As the shots continued without ceasing, Fletcher dove for cover. Bullets flew through the building and ripped into walls.

"Fletcher!" He wasn't moving. She tried to stand, but her leg collapsed beneath her.

"Stay down, Leora." Fletcher kept low and crawled over to her. "I couldn't see who's doing the shooting." He sat up beside Ethan. "How are you feeling?"

"Like I am lucky to be alive." Ethan grinned at his friend. "The last thing I remember was us trying to get away, and I was shot."

Fletcher's troubled gaze met Leora's before he responded. "We were captured." He briefed Ethan on what had happened and about Bowman's threat.

"How did you get loose?" Ethan closed his eyes as if the very effort of asking had drained his strength.

"Jade Powell. She cut us free. We thought she was working for Bowman." Fletcher shook his head. "Bowman ordered her to kill us, only she told us she was working for the FBI. She's trying to find Tanner." He told Ethan what Bowman had said about Tanner.

"Tanner's in real trouble." Ethan looked at Leora. "He has something that can put Bowman in jail for a long time."

Leora shivered at hearing their thoughts confirmed. "Like what?"

Ethan shook his head. "I'm sorry, he didn't tell me."

While Leora tried to figure out what Tanner might have taken, the door flew open. Jade stumbled inside the building and slammed the door shut. She'd barely taken a couple of steps before she collapsed to the floor and grabbed for her leg.

"She's been shot." Fletcher ran to assist. Before he reached her, the door opened again, and Bowman, along with several armed men, charged inside, their weapons raised.

"So, you're the traitor." Ignoring Fletcher's attempts to stop him, Bowman grabbed Jade's arm and hauled her to her feet. Jade shrieked as she was forced to put pressure on her injured leg. "You'll pay for this."

Fletcher once more tried to come to Jade's assistance, but several of the men pointed their weapons at him.

"Take care of them. Now!" Bowman shouted at one of his men. "You're coming with me," he snarled at Jade. "You and Tanner can share the same grave." Bowman forced Jade toward the door while she fought to free herself.

Several men headed toward Leora and Ethan while the man closest to Fletcher aimed his weapon at Fletcher's head.

A weapon went off. Leora squeezed her eyes shut and threw herself over Ethan's body to protect him from the fatal shot. More shots rang out.

The shooting continued, but she was still alive.

Someone tapped her shoulder. Leora flinched away. "Ma'am, it's okay. You're safe now. My name is Deputy Megan Clark. I'm here to help."

Leora slowly looked up. Megan stood beside her. Help had arrived. Relief flooded her as she glanced around the room. Another man dressed in civilian clothes was handcuffing Bowman. The rest of Bowman's men were also being restrained.

Soon, the room was filled with law enforcement and EMTs.

"Let's get your injuries looked after," the female deputy said to Ethan and motioned over several medical personnel.

Fletcher came to sit beside her while two paramedics attended to Ethan.

Leora reached for his hand. "Tanner." She was so worried for her brother.

"The officers have found him," Megan told them.

"I want to go to him."

Fletcher helped her to her feet.

The paramedic finished treating Ethan. "We'll transport him to the hospital now." Ethan's gurney was raised, and two medical personnel rushed him outside to a waiting ambulance.

"Let me have a look at your leg." The female paramedic dropped her bag and waited for Leora to sit.

"I have to find my *bruder*. He needs me."

"It will only take a moment." The paramedic didn't give her the opportunity to refuse. Leora reluctantly lowered herself to the floor. The woman worked quickly to stop the bleeding and bandage the wound. "How does it feel?"

Leora stood and tested the leg. "Much better."

With Fletcher's arm around her waist, they headed for the door and stepped outside. Jade was nowhere in sight. Fletcher led Leora toward the place where numerous law enforcement personnel had gathered. An ambulance, lights flashing, was parked nearby.

"Oh, no," Leora whispered as they neared what appeared to be an open grave. "They buried him."

Leora couldn't imagine Tanner's terror. She remembered how Tanner had been trapped in a collapsed mine when he was only a kid. He'd been stuck there for hours before *Mamm* and *Daed* found him.

Fletcher held her close while several police officers lifted an unconscious Tanner from the shallow grave. As soon as he was above ground, the EMTs went to work.

"Please don't let him die," she breathed.

"He's stable, but he's lost a lot of blood. We've

got to get him to the hospital right away," the EMT said in a grave tone.

"I'm going with him." Leora looked into Fletcher's eyes. "He needs me."

"Go. I'll ride in with the sheriff."

She reached for his hand and held it for the longest time, their gazes tangling.

"Ma'am, we have to go," one of the medical personnel called out from the back of the ambulance.

She reluctantly let Fletcher go. The paramedic helped her into the vehicle and climbed in beside her before shutting the door.

Once they were inside, the driver hit the siren and they drove away from the building.

The lead paramedic continued to work on Tanner while Leora looked on, terrified by how still her twin remained. She clutched her hands tight in her lap and begged *Gott* to let her twin live.

Suddenly the machines attached to Tanner sounded alarms.

"He's crashing," The paramedic grabbed the paddles. "Clear." He worked frantically to save Tanner. Leora looked on in horror as it took several attempts before Tanner stabilized. "I have sinus rhythm." The man studied the monitors attached to Tanner.

"Is he going to be *oke*?"

The EMT laid the paddles down and turned to her. "He has multiple gunshots. It looks like he's been beaten, as well. He's in critical condition, but the doctors at the hospital are some of the best trauma doctors around. He'll be in good hands." The man smiled compassionately. "Pray. He needs your prayers."

And she did. For the rest of the short trip to the hospital, Leora prayed for her *bruder.*

They arrived at the emergency entrance. Tanner was rushed from the ambulance while Leora tried to keep up. The paramedic ran down Tanner's injuries to the doctor on call. "This is his sister." He indicated Leora.

"Is your brother allergic to anything?" the doctor asked her.

She tried to bring her chaotic thoughts into focus. "*Nay*—no. At least not that I'm aware of."

Tanner was rushed into one of the exam rooms. Leora followed the wealth of medical personnel inside and watched as they took an X-ray and quickly assessed his internal injuries.

"Looks like one of the bullets nicked his spleen. He's bleeding internally. He needs emergency surgery. Let's go, people."

Within a matter of seconds, Tanner was wheeled from the room.

Leora struggled to keep up. No matter what, she wasn't about to leave Tanner. She stepped onto the elevator with them. Tension filled the space. Her *bruder* was in serious trouble.

When the elevator doors opened, the team rushed Tanner to surgery. One of the nurses stopped her before she could follow.

"I'm sorry, ma'am, but this is as far as you can go. He's going into surgery. It will take several hours. There's a waiting area right over there. As soon as we have word about your brother's condition, I'll come tell you." The woman smiled sympathetically. "Your brother is in the best possible hands."

Leora managed a nod.

The nurse squeezed her arm and turned to head through the double doors.

Leora let go of a shaky breath and walked over to the rows of chairs set up along one wall. She couldn't believe this was happening. Couldn't believe what they'd gone through so far.

She twisted her hands together and thought about Bowman. From the man's desperate actions, she believed whatever Tanner had taken would prove Bowman was a criminal.

When she couldn't sit still any longer, Leora rose and hobbled to the restroom. The reflection of the woman staring back at her in the mirror was startling. Her face was streaked with mud—skin appeared almost translucent. Dark shadows marred each eye.

She bit down on her trembling lip. They'd almost died. Ethan and Tanner were in serious condition. All because of someone's greed.

Leora unwound her red hair caked with mud and did her best to remove the mud and pin it in place again before washing her face. Once she'd straightened her dress, she surveyed her reflection in the mirror again. It was the best she could do, but there was still no getting around the truth—she had been through something life altering, and it had taken its toll on her body.

A wave of light-headedness swept over her. Leora grabbed the sink and closed her eyes. She couldn't faint. Not now.

When the moment passed, she opened her eyes and pulled in several steadying breaths before leaving the room.

As she headed back to the waiting area, she wondered if Fletcher had arrived yet. And how was Ethan faring?

Help him, please, Gott. *Don't let him pay for these awful men's crimes.*

Leora poured a cup of coffee, which had probably been sitting for hours, and returned to her seat. It had been hours since she'd eaten or drank anything. The coffee burned its way down her throat and into her stomach, where it churned up acid. She set the cup down beside her chair and stretched her injured leg out in front of her. She was so tired. Once this was over and her *bruder* and Ethan and Fletcher were *oke*, she would sleep for hours.

Someone headed toward her down the long corridor. Fletcher. She recognized him immediately and rose unsteadily.

She'd started toward him when the room began to spin. Fletcher, seeing that she was in trouble, rushed to her side.

"I'm *oke*," she whispered unsteadily, grabbing for his hand as everything turned dark and she collapsed into his arms.

THIRTEEN

Fletcher scooped her up into his arms and rushed toward the nurses' station. "Help me, please. She fainted."

"I need a gurney here." The nurse on duty gave the order to another medical personnel standing close. Both sprinted around the station to assist.

Leora was taken from his arms, placed on a gurney, and then hustled down the hall toward an exam room.

"Are you family?" the same nurse asked as he started to follow.

He slowly shook his head. "I'm her friend." The word didn't feel adequate enough for what he felt for her.

"Then I'm going to have to ask you to wait here. When we know what's wrong, we'll tell you what we can."

Fletcher's fuzzy thoughts remembered her condition. "She has—had—cancer." He told her about what Leora had said.

"That's very helpful. Thank you for telling us. I'll let the doctor know." She disappeared down the hall, and all Fletcher could do was stare after her.

He couldn't lose Leora. Not after he'd found hope again in her.

Fletcher paced the hallway, waiting for word.

From behind two double doors, a man in scrubs came his way. The doctor looked around. "I'm looking for Tanner Mast's sister?"

Fletcher told him about what happened to Leora. "Look, I know you're not supposed to tell me anything since I'm not family, but Tanner's sister is a close friend and she's just been rushed into care."

The doctor sighed. "You're right, I'm not supposed to tell you. But… I'm afraid Tanner is critical. We've taken out his spleen, and we think we've stopped all of his internal bleeding, but he's in a coma due to his brain swelling. He took a nasty blow to the head."

"Is he going to make it?" He didn't know Tanner, but he couldn't imagine how hard it would be for Leora to lose him.

"It's too soon to tell," the doctor said. "He's been moved to the ICU. I'm sorry I don't have better news. I'll go check on the sister's progress and let you know how she's doing."

Fletcher couldn't get a response out.

The doctor disappeared in the direction Leora had been taken while Fletcher continued to stare at one spot and count off each second in his head until he returned.

"How is she?" Fletcher hurried toward the doctor.

"She's going to be fine. Apparently, she was severely dehydrated, and the stress of what she's gone through has taken its toll. But she will be okay. Would you like to see her?"

Relief swept over him. "Yes, I would. Thank you, Doctor."

The man led him to a row of rooms and stopped beside one. "She's resting. Try not to tire her out."

Fletcher nodded and hurried inside.

Leora was sleeping. Probably the best thing for her right now. He pulled up a chair beside her bed and took her hand in his while his thoughts swirled around everything that had happened. Immediately upon Sheriff Collins and Fletcher's arrival, they'd been apprised of Ethan's condition. Though still in surgery, the doctor had assured them Ethan would survive his injuries. Fletcher had left to check on Leora and to find out about Tanner's condition, only she'd fainted in his arms.

So much pointless violence had happened. It made him angry that Bowman and his men had gone to such lengths to cover up their crimes, and Fletcher still had no idea what those were.

He glanced out the window, watching the occasional person walk by. He leaned forward and studied Leora's pretty face. She'd been through so much. After surviving cancer twice, now this.

Leora moaned softly. She slowly opened her eyes and saw him. She tried to sit up.

"Nay." He gently urged her not to move. "It's best if you stay where you are. You fainted."

She raised her hand to her forehead. "I can't believe this happened. Tanner." Her eyes shot to his. "Is he…?"

Fletcher dreaded telling her about her twin's condition. "He's alive, but it's serious, Leora."

She didn't blink. "How serious?"

"He's in a coma." He told her what the doctor had said.

"I want to see him." She threw back the covers.

"Leora, this is not a *gut* idea. Not yet. Take it easy for a little bit longer."

She stubbornly shook her head. "I can't. Tanner needs me." She swung her legs over the side of the bed and immediately closed her eyes while clasping her head.

A nurse entered the room. "What's going on here? You are supposed to be resting, miss. Please, get back in bed."

"I can't. I have to see my *bruder.*"

Fletcher told the woman about Tanner. "Please, she's very worried about him."

The nurse slowly agreed. "All right, but you have to do it in a wheelchair, and you have to go with your fluids. Hang on a second. I'll get the chair."

Leora gripped the edge of the bed. Soon, the nurse returned with a wheelchair and helped her into it. "I'll push. You will need to push the IV stand."

Fletcher gladly agreed. He grabbed it and kept pace with the nurse.

Soon, they reached the ICU unit. Fletcher held the door open for Leora. They went inside and over to Tanner's room.

"Okay, I'll come check on you in a couple of minutes," the nurse told Leora before she looked at Fletcher. "If she needs anything, come get me."

Fletcher nodded.

"He looks so still," Leora whispered.

Fletcher pulled up a chair beside her. "The doctors think they stopped all the internal bleeding, but time will tell. He's in the best place he can be."

She turned her face toward him. "I'm so sorry you had to go through this."

He shook his head. "Don't be. I'd do anything for Ethan and for you."

She searched his face before nodding. "How is Ethan?"

"The doctor said he should be fine." Fletcher spotted their nurse talking to another. "I'm going to see if I can find out the latest on Ethan's condition." He went over to the nurse and asked her about Ethan.

"I can check on him for you." The nurse left the ICU, and Fletcher returned to Leora, who continued to watch her *bruder*.

Together they sat in silence, but it was *oke*. He was happy to wait here with her.

When the nurse returned, she gave them good news on Ethan's condition. "Your friend's going to be fine. He is awake and talking. I told him what had happened with your brother. He understands you will be here for a while."

"You should go be with him. I'll stay with my *bruder*."

Fletcher shook his head. "I'd rather stay with you."

The nurse's attention passed between them, and she smiled. "Excuse me." She stepped away.

"It could take some time before Tanner wakes. Ethan needs you. I promise, I'll be fine."

Though he hated leaving her, Fletcher agreed. "All right. I'll check on Ethan and be back soon." He rose and then leaned down and kissed her cheek. "Rest."

When he clasped her shoulder, Leora covered his hand with hers and smiled up at him. The hope he saw in her smile filled him with assurance.

Fletcher left the ICU, found the elevator and rode it down to Ethan's floor. He found his friend's room. Sheriff Collins and two other men in civilian clothes were there, as well.

Ethan spotted him in the doorway and grinned. "Come in, brother. We were discussing what happened."

"I'm glad to see you sitting up." He stopped beside Ethan's bedside.

Ethan laughed and then flinched and grabbed at his injury. "I'm happy to be upright. How's Tanner?"

"Still in a coma. The doctor said the next forty-eight hours will be critical."

Ethan's expression sobered. "Aw, Tanner." He shook his head. "He's strong. And he's been through worse. I tried to find him after we got cut off from each other once we escaped the farmhouse."

He was talking about Sam's place. Fletcher and Leora had been correct. Both Ethan and Tanner had been there at one time.

Sheriff Collins introduced the two men to Fletcher. "Special agents Thomas and Duncan. They work with Jade Powell."

"How does the FBI fit into what was happening?" Fletcher asked. He recalled Jade telling him she'd been working undercover in Bowman's organization.

Agent Thomas responded. "Powell has been working to break up a smuggling ring for several years now. We had no idea how widespread it was. It appears Zeke Bowman has been using his connections abroad to smuggle dangerous contraband like drugs into our country using fake vases and pottery, where he hides them inside."

Fletcher's eyes widened. "You're kidding."

Agent Thomas smiled. "I am not. Thankfully, Jade had worked her way into Bowman's crew and gained his trust. But she still didn't have enough evidence to take Bowman down. She was close until Bowman went after Tanner and Ethan, and everything went south." He blew out a breath. "You see, Jade not only served in Afghanistan with Ethan and Tanner, but she had also once been Tanner and Leora's neighbor in the Ruby Valley."

Fletcher couldn't believe what Thomas had said. Jade knew Tanner from their childhood. Why hadn't Leora recognized her? He asked the agent as much.

"Jade changed her appearance dramatically and her name was Jaden not Jade back then, so it stands to reason, Leora wouldn't recognize her right away." Thomas paused briefly before adding, "We were able to confiscate the crates, and we now have the evidence we need, thanks to Jade's hard work. And when Tanner is awake, we're hoping he'll be able to direct us to where he hid the information he'd gathered on Bowman. Not that it matters. We have enough evidence to arrest Bowman and his crew already."

Fletcher's head swam with all the details.

"By the way, Ethan," Sheriff Collins said, "we have Molly, and she's safe. We were at your property when the call came in from the station owner. There had been a report of shots being fired inside the wilderness. Your place is close, so I went to speak with you about it. The FBI showed up and reported what their agent had told them. We headed into the woods and ran into Molly. She was trying to reach your house."

The dog had obeyed Fletcher's command and had been trying to get them help.

"Anyway, I had the vet, Dr. Mullins, examine her," Sheriff Collins said. "She had an injury to her head, and she was shot, but it was superficial."

"Thank you, my friend." Ethan shifted his attention to Fletcher. "I'm sorry I got you all in the middle of this—"

Fletcher didn't let him finish. "Don't. You'd have my back, too. I know you would."

Ethan inclined his head.

"If you are feeling up to it, can you tell us what happened? How did you become part of the case?" Agent Thomas waited for Ethan to speak.

"It was actually because of Tanner's sister, Leora. She reached out to me when she couldn't get in touch with her brother and after some men broke into her home. I went to find Tanner. I contacted Zeke Bowman, who told me Tanner had quit, and he had no idea where he'd gone."

"You didn't believe him, I take it," Agent Duncan said.

"Exactly. There was something in the way he said it that didn't sit right with me, so I went to Bowman's headquarters and confronted him. He appeared gracious enough, and he certainly knew the right words to say. Anyway, I left, and then I waited to see what he would do. It didn't take long for him to snap into action. He left the building, and I could tell he was nervous, so I followed him."

Fletcher wasn't surprised Ethan had willingly put himself in danger.

"Bowman drove to this deserted building. He was there for only a short period of time, but I knew something was going on because he had a man guarding the place. Once Bowman left, I disarmed the guard and found Tanner. I got him out and brought him back to my house. Tanner was in bad shape. Bowman's men had beaten him pretty badly. I bandaged him up and waited for Tanner to be able to tell me what he'd gotten himself entangled in when Bowman's people forced their way into my home. They held us at gunpoint and searched the place, looking for what Tanner had on them. I'm guessing Zeke's people must have tracked Tanner through his phone." He sighed deeply and closed his eyes briefly.

"I'd say that's a good possibility. How did they get the jump on you and your security system?" Sheriff Collins asked. Fletcher had been surprised by this, as well. Ethan was always acutely aware of safety.

"Good question. I think they somehow scrambled the security system because I never knew they were there until they were right on top of us. There was no time to reach the panic room."

"But how did they get past Molly?" Fletcher wondered aloud.

Ethan shook his head. "I'm guessing Molly was outside when they came up. They probably knocked her out. She was nowhere in sight when they forced me and Tanner out of the house. From what Fletcher said, Bowman's men must have come back to the house, hoping that we might have returned to it after Tanner and I escaped Sam. I don't know how they had the panic room code other than they may have gotten it out of Tanner by torturing him." Ethan's jaw tightened. "They'd beaten him pretty badly."

Fletcher's mind whirled from hearing everything Bowman had put his friend and Tanner through. Not to mention himself and Leora.

"As soon as Tanner is awake, we'll need to hear his side of the story, as well as have him tell us where he hid the evidence he gathered on Bowman," Agent Thomas told them all.

Leora must be going crazy with worry for Tanner. He didn't want to let her go through the fear alone a moment longer. "*Bruder,* I'm happy you are awake and doing well, but I need to check on Tanner. Leora is all alone."

"Go and be with her. She's been through so much," Ethan told him. "Tell Leora I'll be praying for Tanner."

Fletcher inclined his head and headed out the door. He was grateful Ethan was safe and Bowman and his goons had been captured. The rest of the details could be sorted out by Sheriff Collins and the team of FBI agents. Now that the danger had passed, his thoughts were all for Leora. There was no denying he cared about her. He'd stopped believing in love after Catherine, but Leora had made him see the truth. Catherine wasn't his future. She was.

Could he risk trusting her with his heart? He wanted to try.

Fletcher rode the elevator up to ICU and headed toward Tanner's room.

As he neared, he noticed Leora had changed out of the hospital gown she'd had on earlier and into her own clothes. She held her *bruder*'s hand while she bowed her head. She was praying. He stopped and watched her. All the doubts he'd held in his heart were lifted when he realized above helping her find Tanner and Ethan, *Gott* had brought them together for a reason.

As he neared, she raised her head to him.

He stopped beside her and clutched her shoulder. "How is he?"

She shook her head. "He's still unconscious. I'm worried, Fletcher."

He sat beside her and took her hand. "Your *bruder* is strong, and he has the best medical staff helping him. He has you…and me. *Gott* hears prayers, Leora. He will hear ours and bring Tanner back to you."

Tears filled her eyes, and she clutched his hand tight. "I pray you're right."

He struggled for something to say to make her feel better. "Are you hungry?" It had been hours since they'd last eaten anything—probably the chips at the station. Stepping away for a second to take her mind off Tanner's condition would do her *gut*.

She shook her head. "I can't even think about food."

The nurse came over to check on Tanner. "His vitals are stable. A good sign." She patted Leora's arm. "I'm praying for him." She left them alone.

"I wish he would wake up." She pushed out a deep, long sigh and rubbed her hand across her eyes. Leora appeared ready to drop. They'd been tromping through the woods for a long while without any rest.

"He will, soon. I know he will. Let's step outside for a second and get some coffee. We'll come right back," he added before she could protest.

She slowly nodded and rose. "You're right. Tanner will be *oke* for a moment."

Together, they walked from the room.

"How is Ethan? I've been so worried about Tanner I almost forgot to ask."

Fletcher reached for her hand. It felt as natural as his next breath. "He's awake and talking."

Her smile lit up her face. "That's *gut* to hear."

Fletcher's heart soared with love for her, but now was not the right time to tell her the desires of his heart.

They'd reached the waiting room and he

poured coffee. He also noticed a box of donuts and put a couple on a plate. "It's better than nothing and we both need to eat something."

She actually smiled. "They do look tasty. I hadn't realized how hungry I was."

Fletcher put another donut on the plate, and they headed back to the ICU.

Leora stopped outside the room. "Do you mind if we stay here for a minute longer? We can still see Tanner."

His heart went out to her. "Not at all." He thought about her injured leg. "Do you want to sit? There are a couple of chairs."

"I'd rather stand." She continued to watch her sleeping *bruder* while she sipped her coffee.

He held out the plate of donuts. Leora picked one up and bit into it. She closed her eyes. "This is the best thing I've ever eaten."

Fletcher chuckled at her enjoyment. "And I'm not normally a fan of donuts." He noticed a crumb on her cheek and brushed it away, his fingers lingering.

She was so beautiful. As he looked into her eyes, everything he felt for her was there for her to see.

Leora searched his face before reaching for his hand. "Everything happens for a reason. We believe such in our faith. *This* happened for a reason, too."

He swallowed several times. "I never thought I'd feel this way again," he whispered softly. "Never thought..." He stopped. He'd promised himself he wouldn't bring it up yet.

She slowly let him go. Her huge eyes fixed on his held sadness. "I can't do this now."

Those words broke something inside him. Had he been wrong?

The sound of hurried footsteps inside the ICU grabbed Fletcher's attention. Something was happening. Half a dozen different medical personnel rushed toward Tanner.

Leora limped toward her *bruder*.

Fletcher forgot about his broken heart and followed.

"What's happening?" she asked frantically.

Fletcher looked at the wealth of people around Tanner and realized what was happening.

"He's awake."

Leora's startled eyes were glued to her *bruder*. Several of those gathered around made room for her, and she stepped closer to Tanner while Fletcher hung back.

She covered her mouth with her hand. "You're awake."

Tanner managed the tiniest of smiles. "I am."

Her *bruder* had lived. Despite the awful things he'd been through, Tanner was alive.

Gott had spared Tanner's life. All she wanted

to do was to hug him and reassure herself this was real. They'd all survived what had appeared hopeless.

"How did you get here?" Tanner asked in a croaky voice.

Leora didn't know where to begin. "I came when I couldn't reach you. Didn't Ethan tell you?" She regretted the words immediately when it sounded as if she were scolding her injured *bruder*.

His brow wrinkled. "Oh, yeah, he did. Sorry, it's been some really bad days."

Several men entered the room. She recognized the sheriff from the building in which they'd been rescued, along with some of the others with him.

The doctor on duty saw them, as well. "He needs rest. I'm afraid all your questions will have to wait, gentlemen."

The sheriff nodded. "I understand. We're happy to wait. We have most of the story from Ethan, but we'd like to get yours as soon as you're able," he told Tanner. "Until we're certain we've got all the players in custody, I'd like to have one of my people stationed outside the ICU."

Sheriff Collins smiled briefly at Leora and motioned Fletcher outside.

"Can I sit with him?" Leora asked the doctor.

The man gave his consent. "Don't tire him out, though. He's been through a lot, and we don't want him to have any setbacks." After the doctor finished checking Tanner's vitals once more, he and the rest of medical staff stepped away.

She reached for Tanner's hand. "I'm so happy you're *oke*."

Tanner grinned weakly. "Me, too, but I have a feeling you have a story of your own to tell me." He held her gaze. "Who is the man with you?"

Leora's cheeks grew warm. "Fletcher Shetler. He's Ethan's business partner."

Tanner's attention went to where Fletcher and the sheriff talked. "Really? Ethan's friend. He spoke about Fletcher and his brother Mason a lot." Tanner stopped and closed his eyes briefly.

"You need to rest. We can talk more about it when you're feeling better."

Tanner opened his eyes. "I'm okay, and I'd like to talk for a bit."

Leora was torn between hanging on her *bruder*'s every word and wanting to protect him. "Don't tire yourself out."

He remained silent for a long moment. "I never meant for any of this to happen." His words were barely a whisper, but the pain on his face was clear to see. Tanner blamed himself for what had happened.

"Zeke Bowman and his people are in custody. They can't hurt you anymore."

He blew out a relieved sigh. "Thank goodness. Zeke has been smuggling drugs, using his contacts abroad for who knows how long. I had no idea when I took the job this was happening. When I found out, I managed to take photos of the illegal shipments as well as Bowman organizing them. I even got him on tape discussing what he was really shipping in those crates."

"You did *gut*. Along with the evidence you gathered, Bowman is going to jail for a long time."

He shook his head. "I'm just sorry I got you pulled into it. As well as Ethan and Fletcher. This wasn't your battle to fight."

"You could have died, Tanner. I'm so happy we found you in time." She glanced outside to where Fletcher stood talking to Sheriff Collins. He'd been her strong protector. He'd never once left her side in spite of all the terrible things they'd gone through.

"Is there something happening between you and him?"

Tanner's question had her jerking toward him.

"What? Why would you say such a thing?"

Tanner's expression softened. "It's okay, Leora. You deserve some happiness. I see the way you look at him."

Leora looked down at their joined hands. "He helped me find you and Ethan. We've become friends."

Tanner took his time answering. "I know you're worried about the cancer returning, but you can't stop living. You can't fear what might be."

She did her best to keep her voice steady. "It did return, Tanner. My doctor told me he'd got it all, and yet it did return."

"Oh, Leora." The love in his eyes had her fighting back tears. "Yes, it did return, but you don't know it will happen again. And even if it did, do you really want to miss out on living because you're afraid? You don't know how many years you might have to be happy."

Her head knew what he was saying was true, but her heart…oh, her heart. How could she let her heart go there?

"*Gott* loves you, Leora. He would want you to have someone to love and share your life," Tanner said, as if reading her thoughts.

She wanted to believe it, but what if what was happening to her now was *Gott*'s punishment because of what she'd done before.

"It wasn't your fault," he said quietly.

She raised her eyes to Tanner. "I caused them so much pain—and you. I never got the chance to tell them how sorry I was for what I'd done.

But I can apologize to you, like I should have a long time ago. I'm sorry, Tanner. I know my behavior hurt you so much."

He shook his head. "You have nothing to apologize for. You were young and going through your *Rumspringa,* like me."

He sighed deeply. "Leora, you can't keep carrying this guilt around forever. It isn't yours to take on. You didn't set the fire. Someone they knew and trusted did."

This had been the hardest part to accept. Their *Englisch* friend who'd lived near their house. The one they'd shared meals with, worked together in the field with, were friends with his daughters. He had been accused of taking their parents' lives. Yet, even after being convicted of the crimes, he'd refused to admit his guilt. He'd claimed he was being framed until his dying breath.

Not really knowing why their parents had died was one of the reasons that moving beyond their deaths had been hard for both her and Tanner.

"I'm still surprised that Jaden Powell was working for Bowman."

Leora frowned. "Jaden, our former neighbor?" The daughter of the man charged with killing their parents.

Tanner nodded. "She's going by Jade now and working for Bowman."

Leora was surprised she hadn't seen the resemblance before. Jaden had once been her friend. "She isn't working for Bowman, Tanner. She's an FBI agent, and she saved us. And you. Jade found out where Bowman had buried you."

Tanner's surprise was on his face. "I can't believe it," he murmured. The words came out slurred. Tanner closed his eyes.

She patted his hand. "Get some rest. We can talk about it later. You've had enough drama for a while." Leora would find Jaden again and thank her. Perhaps they could catch up. It had been years, and she couldn't imagine how hard life had been for Jaden and her sister, Rose, since their father was convicted of murder and arson.

Tanner grunted something. Soon, he was resting peacefully.

Leora gently untangled her hand and rose, stretching out the kinks from her exhausted limbs.

Outside the ICU, Fletcher talked to the female deputy she'd spoken to earlier.

She left her *bruder* to rest, but she couldn't get what Tanner had said about her finding love out of her head.

Fletcher spotted her and stepped away from the deputy.

"How is he?" He searched her face while she prayed he didn't see the chaos in her heart.

"He's resting. I'm so happy he's doing better. Do you mind if we take a walk? I'd like to see Ethan, as well."

His face relaxed. "Of course." He turned to the deputy and told her where they'd be should something come up with Tanner.

Deputy Clark smiled. "I'll have you paged if there's a change."

"Denki." Fletcher guided Leora toward the elevator. "If you'd like, we can take a walk around the atrium downstairs. It's pretty."

Leora felt the weight of the days spent worrying over Tanner slowly lift. Her *bruder* would have a long road ahead of him to get back on his feet, but he was alive, and she praised *Gott* for this.

"I would love to," she told Fletcher and was happy to ride the elevator in silence.

Once they reached the ground floor, Fletcher pointed to the indoor atrium filled with trees and plants. Benches to sit on were scattered around. It would be the perfect place to come and find comfort when someone you loved was in the hospital.

"This place is beautiful." She found a bench near a small koi pond and sat.

Fletcher sat beside her and studied their surroundings. "I've been here many times when someone I loved was in trouble."

Had he lost someone he loved?

Fletcher caught her surprise. "First I lost my *daed*, then my *bruder* Aaron's first wife passed away here."

"Oh, Fletcher. I'm so sorry." She covered his hand with hers.

He kept his attention on her face. "This is life. We love them for a while, and then we mourn them for a lifetime."

Leora thought about her own parents' deaths. She certainly understood.

"We must live each day of our life. It is a gift."

His words came so close to Tanner's, she couldn't look away.

"Leora, I care about you," he said softly. Her heart reacted to those words immediately. Could she let him say the rest? "And I think you feel the same way about me."

She wouldn't deny it. How could she? Though they'd known each other for just a short amount of time, it didn't matter. In her heart of hearts, she believed *Gott* had brought them together for more than rescuing Ethan and Tanner.

He gathered her hands in his. "I know you're afraid your cancer will return, and I can't make you a promise it won't."

A sob slipped from her trembling lips.

"But even if it does, I will be there with you through it all. And no matter what comes our way, we'll get through it together."

She bit her bottom lip to keep from crying.

"Please take a chance on me, Leora. I know you're scared, but I've got you. I've got you. I love you, Leora. And I want to marry you and be your *mann* if you will have me."

The tears wouldn't be held back any longer, but it was okay because she no longer cared.

"Yes. Oh, yes." She pulled her hands free and put them around his neck. "I love you, too, Fletcher. And I can't wait for us to be married."

He kissed her forehead and held her close.

Leora could hear the steady beat of his heart and was content to stay with him for a while.

"I can't believe what happened," she said with a sigh and was rewarded with the low rumble of his laughter.

"Me, either. My family won't believe it. Mason was once a US Marshal, and he has told me all the things he's witnessed while doing the job. He will be disappointed he missed this."

She laughed and pulled away. "To think those dangerous men met their match with two Amish people."

It was funny to think about.

"Our children won't believe such a tale." The gleam in his eyes made her blush.

Children. She hadn't considered the possibility of being able to have children.

"What if I cannot give you *kinner*?" It would break her heart to disappoint him.

"No, Leora. Don't. Whatever *Gott* choses for us will be exactly what we need. Whether it is a houseful of *kinner* or you and I to grow old together. It will be all we need."

She believed him, but she would pray for a family of their own. Children to follow in their *daeds*' footsteps and carry on the family name.

"Do you want to go see Ethan now?" he asked softly.

She did, but everything was so perfect, she didn't want to break the spell. "Soon. For now, I just want to sit here with you in this beautiful place and forget about all the ugly things that happened. This is a *gut* place. It should be for *gut* memories."

He tugged her into his arms once more. "I agree. We'll stay here for as long as you want."

She leaned against the man who had changed her heart and couldn't believe how much her life had transformed in such a short amount of time.

What others had used for bad, by threatening Tanner and Ethan, *Gott* had turned around and brought blessings into the lives of two people who had suffered so much.

EPILOGUE

Eighteen months later...

"You should relax, my love," Fletcher told his wife, who had been unable to focus on the magazine in her lap since she'd picked it up. "Everything will work out fine, you'll see."

She closed the magazine and placed it back onto the table where the others rested. "I'm trying, but it is so hard, this waiting. Why is it taking so long?"

His insides were knotted with fear, and yet he couldn't show her. "They're busy." He wondered if Leora realized she hadn't let go of his hand since they'd entered the doctor's office.

"How can you be so calm?" The little frown between her brows made him smile.

"Because everything is going to be *oke*." Yet the churning in his gut didn't agree with his words.

"But you can't know for certain." There was

a hopeful look in her eyes. It made him want to do whatever he could to make the waiting easier.

"I can because I believe *Gott* will bless us with a *gut* report."

The exasperated look in her eyes had him grinning. He understood why she had doubts. She'd gone through two different bouts with cancer. But he believed *Gott* would not have brought them together after they'd gone through so much only to tear them apart.

Gott wouldn't let this happen.

Tanner had recovered from his injuries fully and had stayed on in West Kootenai for the time being to be close to his sister. And Ethan— Well, Ethan being Ethan had barely waited until his wounds had healed to continue training his dogs. Jade and her sister, Rose, had become reacquainted with Leora and Tanner, and they had forged a friendship even stronger than before.

Though Leora had hated leaving Martha Cooper behind, they had kept in touch through letters. Martha had written recently to say she'd found another young woman to be her apprentice. According to Martha's letters, the young woman was working out *oke*, even though Martha still missed Leora a lot.

Fletcher and Leora had visited Martha when they'd moved Leora's great-aunt and -uncle to West Kootenai so that Leora could spend more time with them. Fletcher had built them a *dawdi haus* on his property.

"I wish they would call my name," his wife said once more. "I want to get this over with."

This was her annual six-month checkup. For each one before now, she'd received a clean bill of health, yet this one was different. Leora hadn't been feeling well for weeks. At first, she'd thought it was a cold, but then it lingered enough that she'd made her checkup appointment early.

"It will happen soon enough." She looked at him once more, and he tried not to show her the fears in his heart. He couldn't lose her. She was the one he'd been waiting for through one bad breakup.

The door opened near the check-in station and Leora's gaze jerked toward it.

"Thank you, Mrs. Fleming. We'll see you in a year." The nurse walked the woman out into the hall.

Leora's disappointment descended like a dark cloud, and he gathered her in his arms. "Soon," he whispered against her forehead.

But as he watched the clock on the wall, his own frustration grew. The appointment had been scheduled for two o'clock. It was now almost three and, with each ticking second, he was getting worried.

When he was about to go check at the station,

the door opened and one of the women smiled at them. "The doctor is ready for you now. Follow me." She held the door open.

Fletcher grabbed Leora's hand, and they stepped through.

"Right this way," the woman told them, leading the way past a hall lined with exam rooms to the doctor's office. She waited for them to step inside. "Dr. Henderson will be with you shortly," she said before exiting.

"More waiting," Leora whispered.

She and Fletcher sat. He'd been here many times in the past with Leora. The photos of the doctor's degrees, his family, were familiar enough he could almost recite every word on the parchments.

Leora clutched her hands tight.

Please, Gott, let us have gut *news.*

The prayer cleared his head when the door behind the desk opened, and Dr. Henderson came into the room.

"Sorry to keep you both waiting." He held a folder in one hand and shook theirs with the other before claiming his seat.

He opened the folder.

"Is it bad news, Doctor?" Fletcher blurted when the doctor was strangely silent, and he couldn't stand the waiting any longer.

"Fletcher," Leora exclaimed.

Dr. Henderson smiled. "No, it is not bad news at all. Quite the opposite. It's not often I get to give my patients such wonderful news, but I am happy to be able to tell you that you are still cancer free."

Fletcher frowned. "This is good news, but…"

It's not often that I get to give my patients such wonderful news.

The doctor chuckled. "You're right, there is more." He glanced between Fletcher and Leora before giving them the rest. "You're pregnant."

Fletcher's expression froze on his face. He looked at the doctor as if he wasn't sure he'd heard him correctly. "Did you say…?"

Dr. Henderson nodded. "I did. You are pregnant. Leora, you and Fletcher are going to be parents. Congratulations."

Leora slowly turned her head toward Fletcher. Tears hovered in her eyes. That's when he lost it, too. All the emotions leading up to this glorious news came flooding out with her tears. He gathered his *fraa* in his arms and wept with her. "We are going to have a baby."

Leora's shoulders quaked. "We are and I'm so happy."

He was, too.

"Hey, you two—this is a happy time. No more tears." Dr. Henderson's kindly voice interrupted the emotional moment.

Fletcher slowly let her go and wiped his eyes.

"You're right. But they are tears of happiness. We were expecting different news than this."

The doctor inclined his head. "I can understand. But you're healthy, and there should be no problem. This is a time of celebration, my friends. So, go and celebrate. Tell your family the news. Enjoy each moment of this wonderful time."

Fletcher wiped at his eyes again and rose. "We will. This is a miracle, and we will treasure it always."

The doctor rose, as well. "Yes, it is."

Fletcher turned to his wife. "Let's go home."

She beamed up at him. "Let's go home."

Fletcher held his wife's hand as they passed the women up front.

He was trembling all over as they left the doctor's office. He glanced around at the passing foot traffic outside the building before he remembered he'd parked the buggy around the side.

Fletcher headed for it and patted the mare's head without really realizing what he was doing.

Leora entered his line of vision, snapping him out of his daze.

"We're going to be parents," she whispered with a look of pure joy on her face. "Can you believe it?" She started laughing, and he joined in.

"I can't." He couldn't stop smiling and laughing because he was so happy.

He lifted her into his arms and twirled her

around, right there in the parking lot beside the doctor's office for everyone to see.

And he didn't care because he was the happiest he'd ever been.

When they'd left for the appointment, he'd tried his best to have *gut* thoughts. Leora had been worried for days, and he'd wanted to put on a brave front although his gut had been eating him up inside. She had made him realize how important each moment was.

Her expression sobered. "I never thought it would be possible. *Gott* blessed me with you, but I didn't dare let myself believe I would be able to have a *kinna* of my own."

He loved her so much. Fletcher framed her pretty face in his hands. "You will make a wonderful *mamm*. I can't wait to see you and our *sohn*—"

"Or daughter," she inserted, and he smiled lovingly down at her.

"*Jah*, or daughter. I love you, Leora. So much."

"I love you, too." She stood on her tiptoes and kissed him with the love she'd felt in her since the beginning.

Fletcher gathered her close and held her. This woman who had changed his life so much. This woman. His *fraa*.

* * * * *

Dear Reader,

We never know what God has in store for us, or how He can turn our tragedies into triumphs if we trust Him. This is exactly what happened in *Amish Wilderness Survival*.

After losing her parents early on, and then surviving cancer, Leora Mast believes her life has a timestamp on it, and she will never experience the love of a family of her own. But God has a different plan in mind for Leora. We see our tragedies as obstacles, but God sees them as a way to strengthen our faith for future blessings.

When Leora Mast sets out from her home in Colorado to West Kootenai, Montana, to find out what happened to her brother and her good friend, she has no idea how much her life is about to change, or that she will end up finding the love of her life.

God brings Leora and Fletcher Shetler together for a reason, and He carries them through many dangerous situations where they must rely on Him, each other, and a former military dog named Molly to survive. And through the process, they learn that God has a brighter future in store for them…together.

I hope you have enjoyed Leora, Fletcher and

Molly's story. And I hope Leora and Fletcher's journey to find their happy ending will give you hope. No matter what you are going through, you are never alone. God is always there beside you. Ask Him for strength. He'll see you through.

Many, many blessings,
Mary Alford

Get 4 FREE REWARDS!

We'll send you 2 FREE Books plus 2 FREE Mystery Gifts.

FREE
Value Over
$20

Both the **Harlequin® Special Edition** and **Harlequin® Heartwarming™** series feature compelling novels filled with stories of love and strength where the bonds of friendship, family and community unite.

YES! Please send me 2 FREE novels from the Harlequin Special Edition or Harlequin Heartwarming series and my 2 FREE gifts (gifts are worth about $10 retail). After receiving them, if I don't wish to receive any more books, I can return the shipping statement marked "cancel." If I don't cancel, I will receive 6 brand-new Harlequin Special Edition books every month and be billed just $5.49 each in the U.S. or $6.24 each in Canada, a savings of at least 12% off the cover price, or 4 brand-new Harlequin Heartwarming Larger-Print books every month and be billed just $6.24 each in the U.S. or $6.74 each in Canada, a savings of at least 19% off the cover price. It's quite a bargain! Shipping and handling is just 50¢ per book in the U.S. and $1.25 per book in Canada.* I understand that accepting the 2 free books and gifts places me under no obligation to buy anything. I can always return a shipment and cancel at any time by calling the number below. The free books and gifts are mine to keep no matter what I decide.

Choose one: ☐ **Harlequin Special Edition** ☐ **Harlequin Heartwarming**
(235/335 HDN GRJV)   **Larger-Print**
(161/361 HDN GRJV)

Name (please print)

Address   Apt. #

City   State/Province   Zip/Postal Code

Email: Please check this box ☐ if you would like to receive newsletters and promotional emails from Harlequin Enterprises ULC and its affiliates. You can unsubscribe anytime.

Mail to the Harlequin Reader Service:
IN U.S.A.: P.O. Box 1341, Buffalo, NY 14240-8531
IN CANADA: P.O. Box 603, Fort Erie, Ontario L2A 5X3

Want to try 2 free books from another series! Call 1-800-873-8635 or visit www.ReaderService.com.

*Terms and prices subject to change without notice. Prices do not include sales taxes, which will be charged (if applicable) based on your state or country of residence. Canadian residents will be charged applicable taxes. Offer not valid in Quebec. This offer is limited to one order per household. Books received may not be as shown. Not valid for current subscribers to the Harlequin Special Edition or Harlequin Heartwarming series. All orders subject to approval. Credit or debit balances in a customer's account(s) may be offset by any other outstanding balance owed by or to the customer. Please allow 4 to 6 weeks for delivery. Offer available while quantities last.

Your Privacy—Your information is being collected by Harlequin Enterprises ULC, operating as Harlequin Reader Service. For a complete summary of the information we collect, how we use this information and to whom it is disclosed, please visit our privacy notice located at corporate.harlequin.com/privacy-notice. From time to time we may also exchange your personal information with reputable third parties. If you wish to opt out of this sharing of your personal information, please visit readerservice.com/consumerschoice or call 1-800-873-8635. **Notice to California Residents**—Under California law, you have specific rights to control and access your data. For more information on these rights and how to exercise them, visit corporate.harlequin.com/california-privacy.

HSEHW22R3